# The Guns of Gabriel

Blake Durant was one of the crew driving Jay Hurwood's cattle to the railhead at Gabriel. The trail had been hard, but nothing more than he'd expected. Then two murders were committed, right out on the open prairie . . . and suddenly everyone became a suspect.

Because there hadn't been any love lost between Blake and Joe Sowarth, Joe's brother, Lanny, was convinced that Blake was the killer, and figured to even the score any way he could. But there was more going on around Hurwood's trail drive than anyone could imagine, and the only way Blake could clear his name was by finding the real killer . . . and his sinister motive!

# The Guns of Gabriel

Sheldon B. Cole

**A Black Horse Western**

ROBERT HALE

First published by Cleveland Publishing Co. Pty Ltd,
New South Wales, Australia
First published in 1967

© 2019 by Piccadilly Publishing

This edition © The Crowood Press, 2020

ISBN 978-0-7198-3117-1

The Crowood Press
The Stable Block
Crowood Lane
Ramsbury
Marlborough
Wiltshire SN8 2HR

www.bhwesterns.com

Robert Hale is an imprint
of The Crowood Press

leath

# ONE

# OLD WOMAN'S PREDICTION

Blake Durant brought his blue – black stallion, Sundown, up the rise and across a barren stretch to Hap Wheeler's chuck wagon. The old – timer's face brightened as Durant drew up. Wheeler's beard was white with dust and his eyes were strained with weariness and sun – glare. It had been a long haul out of Cheyenne for the old man and although hardly an hour had gone past during which Wheeler hadn't voiced a complaint about some-thing, he had never once directed his complaints at a definite person. He was, Blake had discovered in

5

the three weeks he had been with this outfit, just a grumbler who went his own way and seemed to like it that way.

'Storm's coming up, Hap,' Blake told Wheeler as he stepped out of the saddle and loosely hitched Sundown to the wagon's side. A sharp wind dragged a canvas flap out of Wheeler's hand and slapped it against the old man's drawn face.

Grabbing irritably at the flap, Wheeler grumbled, 'You think I'm so blind, Durant, that I can't see them clouds back there?'

'Be on us within ten minutes,' Blake said, then he eased Wheeler aside, pulled the flap back in place and tied it securely to the rail.

Wheeler, the chore taken out of his hands, checked the lid on his flour box and then, taking off his battered range hat, he slapped it against his thigh. 'Weeks of dust and now mud,' he grumbled. 'A man's loco to the hilt to be in this kind of business. Be better to be propped up on a porch chawin' on handouts.'

Blake released Sundown and looked about for shelter for the black. He saw a hollow not far off from the camp, with a clump of trees affording protection against storm blasts from the south. Accustomed to range camps and long trailing, the black would probably welcome the change from the dust and the heat. Like himself, the horse wel-comed any change. Ground – hitching the big black, Blake Durant removed the saddle, gave the horse a reassuring pat and brought the saddle back and packed it under the rear wheel of the wagon. As he straightened, Dave Crane, the youngest member of the outfit who still had an air of adventure about him, rode briskly up and pointing to the south called out to Wheeler:

'Hap, we've got a storm coming up. Best batten down.'

Wheeler scowled up at the young man and gave a grunt. Crane swung his long legs to the ground and wiped dust from his face. He smiled Blake Durant's way and said, 'Gonna come down in buckets soon. Hell, you can feel it, can't you?'

Blake nodded. He liked Crane. He was inexperi-enced but not too proud to learn. And he learned quickly. He had youth and strength and guts, and he took what came his way in the manner of a man who realized that life was just beginning for him. With Hap Wheeler, Crane was respectful. With the other two hired hands, Joe and Lanny Sowarth, Crane was careful. Blake figured he was smart; he was careful with the two himself.

'Hap, anything I can do for you?' Crane offered, walking to the wagon's side where Wheeler was still checking to make sure they wouldn't be wet when the storm hit.

Wheeler's head lifted sharply. 'Now what in blue blazes would I need you for, young 'un?'

'Just asking, Hap. If you need me, just holler.' Crane removed his hat, raked his sandy hair with his left hand and looked south. 'Be great to get soaked, eh, Durant? Hell, I reckon I could sit in a downpour for a week and still not feel clean. I got dust so deep – buried in me that I'm starting to creak.'

A rumble of thunder came from the south and the three of them looked that way. Two men rode over the rise from that direction and came on fast for the camp. Joe Sowarth, the elder of the two brothers, wheeled in hard against the wagon's side, making Hap Wheeler twist away to avoid the sudden rise of dust. Hap's grumble was lost in the arrival of Lanny Sowarth, who flicked a look over the camp-site, saw Blake's barebacked horse and looked heavily at him.

'You figure to let the rest of us keep that bunch of steers quiet, Durant?'

Blake held his look. 'I don't like sitting in a wet saddle, Sowarth – during rain or after it.'

Lanny Sowarth's gaze shifted until he sighted Durant's saddle packed under the wagon. He gave a derisive snort and looked about for something else to criticize.

'Rangeman with all the answers,' Joe Sowarth said to back up his brother.

But Blake Durant ignored them both and looked skyward. The wind had cooled considerably. He pulled his range coat about his wide, flat shoulders and tucked his yellow bandanna under his collar. Then he stood there, facing the wash of the wind, hearing the movement of the others about him, isolated from them, as his green – eyed look went out across the distance. He had no actual part in this outfit. He had signed on for the last three weeks of the drive because he was headed north anyway, on the drift, going where the trails took him and not caring what his destination was. It had been like that for a long time now, a man who had nobody anywhere, a man with a horse and a gun, his mind on something he wanted, and searched for, a something that was never distinct in outline, ever distant. With him went the memories of happier, fuller days . . . of a woman he'd loved and lost to death. He could not forget and he didn't know if he wanted to forget. So there was just the endless drifting and searching.

The first drops of rain hit his tanned, weathered face. These were but the start of the storm, the full fury of which would not hit for another ten minutes at least. So there was no need to hurry across to Sundown, mount him and ride the fringe of the herd to stop a stampede. He expected at any moment to get a call from either Joe or Lanny Sowarth, a call he would ignore as he had time after time. Jay Hurwood, who owned the herd and had ridden ahead to make arrangements for its sale in Gabriel, had not left anybody specifically in charge, but Blake knew Joe Sowarth was the man most likely to give orders in Hurwood's absence. Blake didn't care. He would do what he had to do.

'What the hell's that?'

The question caused Blake Durant to turn. He saw Joe and Lanny Sowarth still sitting their horses while Dave Crane was unsaddling his mount. Blake followed the direction of the brothers' gazes and saw a rig coming from the north. Dust boiled about its creaking wheels. In the seat, hunched forward against the wind, was an incredibly old woman, whose face, as she drew rein, was a mess of wrinkles, sallow flesh and warts. Her dark eyes took in the bunch of cowhands intently but no emotion whatever showed in her face.

'Who the hell are you?' Joe Sowarth asked.

'An old woman.'

Joe Sowarth glanced at his brother and grinned. 'Hell, I can see that. You'd be older than Moses.

10

THE GUNS OF GABRIEL

Where the hell did you come from – out of some dung heap?'

Still no emotion showed in the old woman's face, but her gaze kept switching about, searching. Then she said, 'I came from Gabriel. I have a long way to go and little food.'

Joe laughed scornfully. 'They pitch you outa town on account of your stink, old woman?'

Her head turned and her eyes bored at Joe. She said nothing but Joe Sowarth shifted uncomfortably under her gaze.

'Leave her be,' put in Dave Crane. 'She ain't doing anybody any harm and you can see she's sick.'

'Sick?' Joe said to the young cowboy. 'Can't you smell the whiskey, boy?'

Hap Wheeler was already loosening a flap and reaching inside the wagon for some provisions. Lanny Sowarth watched him sourly but said nothing. Blake Durant came up then and eased Crane away. He stepped to the rig's side and looked up into the old, withered face. He said:

'There's a storm coming up, ma'am. I think you best come down and get shelter. I'll see to your horse.'

She looked at Durant for a long, silent moment before she shook her head. 'I must go on. The storm will not hurt me. I am part of the wind and the rain and the sun.'

Joe Sowarth gaped at her. 'What's that?'

The old woman ignored him. Looking past Durant, she studied Dave Crane intently before she put out a withered hand and beckoned him with a long, crooked finger. Crane looked uneasily at Durant. When Blake didn't respond to his questioning look, Crane came hesitantly forward.

Taking his hand, the old woman studied Crane's palm and smiled. 'This land is for young people. You must always stand straight. A fat whelp will lick your hand. An unfed whelp will savage you.'

Feeling her grip slacken, Crane withdrew his hand and looked troubled. A louder roll of thunder came from the south. Then the old woman looked into Blake Durant's eyes and smiled again.

'Seek and you will find,' she muttered. 'Every trail is not lonely forever.'

Joe Sowarth, shifted aside by Hap Wheeler as the old – timer packed a parcel of provisions in the back of the rig, grunted impatiently and said, 'What's this damn drivel? We ain't got time to listen to this kind of hogwash. We've got a herd to look after.'

The old woman ignored him and nodded at Hap Wheeler. 'There have been many suns and many moons. But there is still time.'

Hap moved away, looking uncomfortable, and Joe Sowarth swore. The old woman glanced in

Lanny Sowarth's direction finally and after studying his face for a long moment, she shook her head. Lanny's mouth tightened and then the old woman studied Joe, her eyes seeming to sink deeper into her bony face.

'Some come to spoil the harvest,' her voice rang out louder than before. Thunder rumbled and a flash of lightning brightened the darkening sky. The wind came up stronger and flapped her threadbare coat about her thin body as she said, 'Some are born who should not have been.'

Joe Sowarth's face went livid and he straightened in the saddle, glaring down at her. 'You old crone, who the blazes do you think you are?'

'Some things should not be,' she said finally, looking defiantly up at him still.

Joe hissed a curse and shifted a fraction closer. 'Shut down, you old witch!' he snapped. 'I ain't takin' that from you or anybody.'

'Death will flap its black wings and everybody will rejoice,' she taunted him again and this time Joe Sowarth bucked his horse side – on to the rig and reached for her.

But before Sowarth's hand could grab her, Blake Durant worked his horse away. He stood then between Sowarth and the old woman and said quietly:

'Leave her be.'

Joe Sowarth swung his horse around, bringing its head towards Blake's head. Blake put up a hand to keep the horse from hitting him, then he dragged on the reins and slapped his hand down the animal's side. The horse reared, and Joe Sowarth, almost unseated, struggled to quieten the animal before he flung himself out of the saddle at Durant.

Durant caught Sowarth in both hands and sent him crashing to the ground. Lanny Sowarth let out a growl and started to come forward but found his progress stopped by Crane and Hap Wheeler.

Crane said tightly, 'She ain't done anybody any harm.'

Joe Sowarth came off the ground, wiped the dust from his hands and charged at Blake Durant. But Durant again met him with both hands. He grasped Joe's shoulders and then, as the impetus of Sowarth's charge was stopped dead, Blake flung him away again. This time Lanny Sowarth kicked Crane and Hap Wheeler away from him and slid down from his horse. But by then Joe had come to his haunches, his face black with anger; he suddenly dropped his hand for his gun, but Durant drew and had his gun leveled before Joe Sowarth could clear leather. Incredulity filled Joe Sowarth's face as his hand froze on the gun butt. Durant moved away from the rig and saw Lanny Sowarth also going for his gun. He swung his gun and Lanny's hand stopped dead.

'It doesn't have to go any further,' Durant said coolly.

'And it damn better not!' put in Hap Wheeler from the chuck wagon's side.

Both the Sowarth boys glanced his way and saw Hap's gun trained on them. Dave Crane stood absolutely still, his face filled with worry, his hands at his sides.

Heavier rain fell now, and the old woman, looking completely isolated from the trouble brewing about her, picked up the rig reins and said into the blackening sky, 'The way is long for some but short for others.' Then she drove off.

Joe Sowarth rose from the ground and wiped his right hand down his shirt front. He glared furiously at Durant. 'It doesn't end here, Durant, so help me.'

'We've got a herd to look after,' Blake said. 'That's what matters now. Otherwise nobody gets paid.'

Lanny Sowarth stood with his feet planted wide, his inner struggle working lines into his long face. He nodded at Durant and said, 'After the payoff, mister.'

'As you like,' Blake answered, then Lanny eased his brother back against his horse.

Joe scowled at Blake but another nudge from Lanny made him swing onto his horse.

Lanny, again in the saddle, wheeled his horse around and said, 'Joe and I will take the right flank. You and Crane take the left flank, Durant.'

Blake didn't argue. He watched them go off and then motioned for Crane to follow. Hap Wheeler put up his gun and said tightly, 'I'd watch them, Durant.'

Blake nodded at him. Crane got his horse and swung up. Then, breathing a sigh of relief, he headed off to keep the herd quiet. Blake Durant went to Sundown and rode him bare – back out of the campsite. By then the old woman had reached the rim of the slope and slowed. She was sitting perfectly still, a peculiar smile fixed on her fleshless face, her eyes turned towards the sky. The rain was coming down harder now and there were frequent flashes of lightning and loud thunder rolled across the sky.

Hap Wheeler, his mouth pinched tight, stared in the direction of the old woman. Deep worry worked through his mind and he felt a chill run down his spine. He cursed her but immediately withdrew the curse and then he blanked his mind to her. He didn't even want to think of the strange things she had said. He busied himself re – tying the flap of the chuck wagon and then scurried under the wagon and out of the rain.

It was the kind of storm Blake Durant had often experienced in this part of the country. The first light rain gave due warning, but after a few minutes of this the wind began to howl and the black sky scowled down, driving the daylight out of the basin country. Flashes of lightning occasionally lit up huge areas, spooking the cattle. Thunder rolled so close overhead that each crack of it seemed to be driven into a man's head. Durant rode the left flank, leaving Dave Crane to guard the top of the herd. He couldn't see the Sowarth brothers, but he knew their minds would no longer be filled with worries about him. They'd be as he was, buffeted, slashed, stung by hail and driving rain, his horse frequently losing its footing in country that had been a dust bowl earlier but was now sloppy mud.

The cattle milled about continually, and occasionally a frightened steer made a break from the mob. Blake managed to turn several of them back, but three got past him. He didn't make the mistake of leaving his post and trying to catch them. In this weather, steers would not run far unless the whole mob broke into a stampede. Then it would take at least a day to get them together again, and with Gabriel so close, Blake didn't want that chore.

So he worked his line, caring nothing about his own discomfort. Years in the cattle business had fitted him for this and worse. All a man could do was ride out the storm. Lightning cracked and thunder drummed against the hillsides, then the whole prairie was steeped in a strange darkness shot through now and then with thunderbolts, each jagged streak lighting the bellowing herd. Durant kept riding up and down, calling to the cattle. Buffeted and hammered, Durant felt the sting of the rain and hail but tried to ignore it. This would not last long, he told himself, furious though it was. And he was right. As suddenly as the storm had hit, it ended. The darkness lifted and gray light showed the herd to be bedraggled but still close – bunched. Durant rode to where Dave Crane was a forlorn, soaked figure on a horse whose sides were heaving. Durant knew Crane had done his part and more.

He said, 'I'll fetch those few strays. Stick with these until I get back or until you see me on the rise heading back to camp. There won't be any trouble now.'

Crane looked skyward as if not ready to believe him. Sodden, beaten, overburdened with weariness, the young cowhand didn't have it in him to argue. He watched Durant ride off and was glad the big man had been with him during the crisis.

He knew he would have backed off from those tossing threatening steer horns if left alone.

Durant reached the slushy rise and went over it and into a little valley. Here the country was filled with an eerie silence, and the darkness which had so recently filled the prairie hung on. Blake rode through, with Sundown adroitly dodging deadfalls and disturbed rocks. Small rivulets came down from the rocky slopes and washed against Sundown's hocks, making progress more dangerous. Studying the ground in the gloom, Blake Durant found it impossible to pick up the tracks of the three strays. He reached the valley's end and was about to turn back to camp, accepting the loss of the strays as Jay Hurwood would have to accept it. But Sundown, making a slow turn, suddenly stopped, shied back and then lifted his head and neighed in fear.

Durant placed a hand on the stallion's shoulder and gently talked to him. Sundown quietened, but still quivered under Blake. He knew then that something out of the ordinary was close to them, something the big black did not like or understand. Blake looked searchingly about him and finally picked out a dark shape on the crest of the slope. At first it looked like a huge spider, legs outflung in agony, but closer inspection showed it to be the old woman's rig, overturned. Blake slid off Sundown and hurried up the slippery slope. Twice he fell, but after several minutes he reached the horseless rig.

Here on the top of the rise the light was better. It took him only a moment to locate the old woman. She lay in deep mud, her face buried beneath it. Blake drew her out of the mud. Then, after righting the light rig, he put her down on the broken driving seat. It was only then that he saw she had blood on her neck and sunken bosom. He felt for a pulse but found none. Propping her up, he saw that her neck wound had been caused by a bullet fired at close range.

Blake lowered, her to the rig seat and stepped back, disturbed and puzzled. He and Dave Crane had worked the right side of the herd; the Sowarth brothers had worked the left side. So the brothers would have been closer to this section during the storm.

Blake made a thorough search of the area. If horse tracks had been there, the storm had washed them out. Under the howl of the wind and the crashing of thunder, a gunshot would have gone unheard. He returned to the rig, picked up the old woman's body and carried it to Sundown. Placing the frail body over the horse, he climbed up behind it and rode slowly to the rise above the camp.

When Hap Wheeler saw the body draped over the horse, a chill went through him. He came to the front of the chuck wagon as Blake Durant drew rein. Blake dismounted and eased the body off the horse. Hap Wheeler stepped back suddenly and shook his head. His bewhiskered face was white and strained.

'I knew somethin' was gonna happen, Durant! Some of them noises in the storm came from Hades, no mistake.'

Blake placed the body gently against the wagon's side. Then he pulled back the shawl from her neck and Hap Wheeler gasped.

'Shot!' he said. 'Now who in all hell would do a thing like that?'

'That's what we've got to find out,' Blake said. 'It wasn't me and it wasn't Crane.'

Hap continued to gape at him. Then he licked his lips nervously. 'Hell, she didn't do nothin' bad enough to get treated like that. She wasn't really worryin' anybody.'

Blake nodded, then he tidied the old woman's tattered dress as best he could and looked out across the mud. Dave Crane appeared on the rim of the ridge and rode slowly towards them. At the wagon he slipped from the saddle and took off his soaked range hat and began to batter it against his long – limbed legs.

'Don't reckon I want to go through another of them storms for a spell, Durant,' Crane muttered. 'Do you get 'em often in these pants?'

Blake didn't answer. He stood against the chuck wagon's side and stared thoughtfully towards the valley where the Hurwood steers were now quiet. Then Lanny Sowarth, looking uneasily about him, showed up on the rim line. After staring heavily about him, he rode down to the camp and, looking at each man in turn, asked:

'You seen Joe?'

Wheeler looked at Durant and Lanny Sowarth didn't miss the concern in the old man's heavily lined face. A frown rutted his brow.

'What is it?' Sowarth asked gruffly. 'What the hell's happened?'

Durant jerked his head towards the front of the wagon, where Dave Crane, white – faced and shaking, was peering down at the old woman's body. Hearing Lanny Sowarth come up, Crane stepped back quickly and turned to Durant.

Blake watched Lanny Sowarth's face closely and decided he saw genuine surprise. He went to Sowarth, saying, 'I found her in the small valley we decided wasn't big enough to hold the herd when we made camp. The rig was overturned and the horse was gone.'

Lanny Sowarth's face went dark with anger. 'So you three figured things out for yourselves, eh?'

'What we figure is your brother ain't here and a dead woman is,' Hap Wheeler said. 'What do you make of it?'

Blake Durant was quick to say, 'No sense in anybody jumping to conclusions. The light's getting better all the time and soon it'll be good enough for all of us to go look around. But I don't expect that whoever shot her would leave tracks.'

'There are only five of us,' Hap Wheeler put in. 'Durant and Crane were together, so they'd know if it was one or the other. Me, I ain't left here as you can see because I ain't hardly wet. Then there's you, Sowarth, and your brother, who wanted to hurt the old woman before the storm hit.'

Lanny Sowarth glared furiously at Wheeler for a long time before he grated, 'Put what you're sayin' in plain words, old – timer.'

Wheeler straightened his old body and held Lanny Sowarth's gaze. 'I ain't sayin' but what is, Sowarth. You put it otherwise.'

'Why, you blasted – ' Sowarth went for his gun – and found himself looking into the muzzle of

Blake's Colt. Blake's draw had been so fast that Crane gasped in surprise. Sowarth's hand remained on his own gun butt while hatred contorted his lean face.

Blake said, 'None of us know anything and most likely won't until your brother gets back, Sowarth. So we'll leave it be for the moment.'

'I ain't lettin' no whiskered old coot – '

'For now we'd better all quieten down,' Durant said. Then, seeing Lanny Sowarth's hand leave his gun butt he slid his own gun back into leather. He saw that Hap Wheeler had his rifle handy; so, telling Crane to get a shovel, he lifted the old woman's body in his arms and carried it up the clearing to the belt of trees where Sundown had been tethered, before the storm broke.

# TWO

## TWO DEAD

There were no tracks at all near the broken rig. Dave Crane rode a wide circle about the valley, searching again, but Blake Durant and Lanny Sowarth remained close to the rig, neither man speaking, each caught up in his own troubled thoughts. Sowarth continually swept the terrain with his keen gaze, and Blake knew he was hoping for a sign of his brother.

'Coulda been anybody passing through, Durant,' Sowarth said. 'It wasn't Joe. He was with me all the time, just like Crane was with you.'

'I never lost sight of Crane for a minute during the blow, Sowarth. He and I are clear and so is Wheeler.'

Lanny Sowarth glared furiously at him. 'Damn you, Durant, you listen to me! Joe's about some-place, likely fetching back some strays. You gang up on me and him and by hell you'll be sorry you did!'

'The truth is what we want, Sowarth,' Durant said. 'Until we get it, nobody's leaving this area.'

With that, Blake Durant turned Sundown around and rode to where Crane had finally stopped, his face glistening with sweat.

Crane shook his head and muttered, 'It sure is a mystery. If it wasn't for the bullet hole in her, I'd say the storm spooked her horse and she was thrown out and got killed. But there is the bullet hole and no denyin' it.'

Blake made no comment. He looked about him, tall in the saddle, his face expressionless. Suddenly he said, 'Go back and stay with Hap.'

Sowarth was approaching. Crane licked his lips nervously and backed his horse a couple of steps.

'What – what are you going to do, Durant?' Crane asked.

'Keep looking for strays.'

Blake moved Sundown away from Crane and rode slowly along the small, mud – covered valley.

Sowarth joined Crane and growled, 'You run into my brother, keep your mouth shut, Crane. Ain't nobody here gonna say somethin' to him that ain't true.'

'I'd like to know where he is,' Crane said with a touch of defiance in his voice. He thought of the old woman and what had happened to her and an involuntary shudder went through his young, range – trimmed body.

'My brother's out rounding up strays. It's nothing more than that, Crane,' Lanny said severely. 'You got that?' Sowarth brought his horse up hard against Crane's. 'You got it?'

Crane held Sowarth's savage look for a moment, then he pulled his horse clear and rode back to the campsite, where Hap Wheeler was mopping up some water that had leaked into the wagon. To Dave Crane's way of thinking, big trouble was in the offing and he wanted to keep out of it as much as possible. Durant had twice proved he could handle things. As for Hap Wheeler, he was experienced enough to make the right moves. So Crane decided he would watch Wheeler and follow his lead for the time being. The rest would take care of itself – unless there was a serious confrontation between Lanny Sowarth and Blake Durant. If that happened, Dave Crane would back up Durant.

About ten minutes passed and then Durant showed up on the rim of the slope, driving four steers before him. The steers went over the rise and ran for the herd. Durant rode slowly back to the camp. He slipped off Sundown just as Lanny Sowarth came over the rise and walked his horse towards them. He left his horse hitched to the side of the chuck wagon and settled down on a large rock.

Wheeler got a fire going, put on coffee and then began to prepare the evening meal. Blake Durant spent his time rubbing down Sundown while Crane sat behind the chuck wagon, keeping out of the way.

The smell of coffee was wafting over the clearing when Lanny Sowarth and Blake Durant lifted their heads and stared west at the sound of hoofs. A rider came into view, walking his horse. Sowarth jumped to his feet, his face brightening, but a moment later, as Durant joined him, his face darkened.

'Hurwood,' Blake said.

Sowarth moved in front of Blake, his face tightening. Then Blake saw the second horse trailing behind Hurwood's mount. On the second horse was the limp figure of a man draped over the saddle. He had no doubt whatever as to the identity of the man. The clothes, despite the mud on them, were Joe Sowarth's. Lanny Sowarth let out a groan and ran forward, slipping in the mud. Jay Hurwood saw him coming and reined in. Sowarth reached him, ran to the side of the trailing horse and lifted the head of the dead man. A deep groan came out of him, then his head jerked up and his look at Jay Hurwood was full of venom.

Hurwood, seeing Durant, Crane and Wheeler coming, said quietly, 'I found him back in the creek area, Lanny, face down in the wash.'

Lanny's face was white as he pulled his brother's body from the saddle and eased it to the ground. Blake Durant reached the horses and saw the gaping bullet wound in Joe Sowarth's stomach. His shirt was badly torn, as though ripped by clawing, frantic hands.

'Joe! Joe!'

Lanny Sowarth knelt at his brother's side, brushing the thick black hair away from his brother's death – paled face.

Hurwood said, 'He's dead, Lanny. I checked that out first thing. Anybody know what happened?'

Lanny Sowarth came slowly to his feet. He stood there, staring down at his brother, then he wheeled away with a moan of despair.

'Down by the creek, Hurwood, you said?' Lanny swung to Blake Durant and his hand dropped to his gun.

Blake Durant made no move to go for his Colt, although he saw the vicious hatred in Lanny

Sowarth's eyes.

'Down by the creek was where you said you were looking for strays,' Lanny muttered. 'You trailed Joe there and you killed him.'

Jay Hurwood said angrily, 'Lanny, quit that now. We don't want any more dead. I've got a herd to get to Gabriel.'

'Shut up, damn you!' Lanny roared. He had his gun trained on Blake Durant now, but Durant didn't appear unduly worried.

Blake said, very quietly, 'From the time we left the herd, Lanny, I was in plain sight of everybody.'

'Before then, damn you!' Lanny rasped. 'It was before that. You went looking, you said, then you came back with the old crone. Who else did you meet, Durant. I say you met my brother and then you killed him!'

Blake Durant held Lanny's fierce gaze evenly. He saw Jay Hurwood lift his gun from his holster, then he said, 'Lanny, I had no reason to kill your brother.'

Lanny Sowarth straightened, waving his gun wildly. 'No, Durant? How about when Joe said you were in for it as soon as we got these cattle to Gabriel? You were afraid of him, Durant. Joe would've shot your stinkin' guts out and you knew it.'

Blake shook his head. 'He would have had no chance with me, Lanny. I had no reason to kill him and I didn't.'

It was then that Jay Hurwood, leaning forward in the saddle, brought his gun butt down on the back of Lanny Sowarth's head. Sowarth grunted and fired, but the bullet whined harmlessly over Durant's head. Then Lanny slumped to the ground and lay still.

Durant looked at Hurwood, who leathered his gun and said, 'I won't have gunplay in my outfit. Durant, get that gun of his and hand it up. I'll take yours, too – and Crane's. Hap, you get that blunderbuss of yours out of the chuck wagon. There'll be no more gunplay until after we reach Gabriel.'

Blake Durant studied Hurwood intently for a moment before he reached down and plucked the gun from the mud. He turned the butt and handed the Colt up to Hurwood. Hurwood sat back in his saddle. He dropped Sowarth's gun into his saddlebag and extended his hand towards Crane and Durant. Crane passed his gun across without delay, but Blake Durant, lips pursed, hesitated. Hurwood glared at him and said:

'I'm getting that herd into Gabriel at first light, Durant, and nothing is gonna stop me. So, until we break up this camp, nobody is gonna do any killing.

31

THE GUNS OF GABRIEL

We'll just sit about and talk this out and see if we can get to the bottom of it.'

Hap Wheeler, who had been examining the body of Joe Sowarth, came back to them and said clearly, 'I'll get my gun, Jay. I reckon you pulled the right rein on this one.'

Blake Durant suddenly slid his gun free of leather and handed it up. Then he went to where Lanny Sowarth lay, plucked him from the ground and threw him across his shoulder. He carried Lanny towards the camp as Crane got Joe Sowarth's body back onto the saddle of the trailing horse. Then Hurwood, Crane and Hap Wheeler came to the campsite and Hurwood slid out of the saddle. Looking wearily about him, he sighed deeply.

'Pity it had to happen, Durant, but he asked for it. Now what the hell was he talking about, you and Joe gunning for each other?'

Blake told him about the arrival of the old crone and her criticism of Joe Sowarth. When he dismissed the rest of it as inconsequential, Hap Wheeler broke in.

'Sowarth went at Durant and came off badly, so I guess he figured it was time for gunplay. But that didn't do him no more good than the punches he threw and missed with. Durant got a gun on him, quick as you can blink. Then the storm broke and we were busy with other things.'

'And the old woman?' Jay Hurwood asked.

Hap looked at Durant. 'When the storm passed, Durant went looking for strays like Lanny said, but he came back with the old woman, who'd been shot through the neck.'

Jay Hurwood gaped. 'Shot?'

Wheeler nodded and pointed up the clearing. 'Durant and Crane buried her up there: She was a strange one, old as a cliff face and I don't reckon she had kin who mattered. Got right under Joe Sowarth's skin, sayin' the things she did about him. Joe was gonna maul her some, only Durant stopped it. That's what sparked it all off.'

Jay Hurwood looked quickly away as Lanny Sowarth groaned. Bringing his hands to his head, Lanny pushed himself away from the chuck wagon wheel against which Durant had propped him.

'Lanny?' Jay Hurwood moved across to Sowarth, who leaned against the wagon. 'Sorry about that, son, but somebody had to stop you. Seems we got an old woman shot dead and also your brother. Nobody knows what it's all about, so we've got to put our cards on the table and see if we can come up with a sensible explanation.'

A strange gleam came into Lanny Sowarth's eyes. He looked past Jay Hurwood at Blake Durant.

'I know what happened.'

'Let's hear it then,' Hurwood said, turning to look at Durant.

Lanny Sowarth glared at Blake Durant. 'He killed Joe – and I'll get him for it!'

'Durant says he didn't shoot your brother.'

'He's a damned liar!'

Hurwood looked uncomfortably from one to the other and sighed wearily. 'Durant says he went looking for strays and found the old woman shot in the neck. Then he brought her back here to the camp. Now what we've got to work out is the time lapse from when Durant was last seen by one of you and when he showed up here with the old woman. Could he have got down to the creek in that time, killed Joe and then ride back here, pick up the old woman and return to camp?'

Lanny Sowarth frowned heavily. 'He had time,' he said.

'To hell he did,' put in Hap Wheeler. 'Hell, I saw Durant go over that rise between here and the cattle grounds. He wasn't away more'n ten minutes, and as I remember these parts it's a good five miles to the creek.'

'More like six,' Jay Hurwood put in.

Lanny Sowarth struggled to his feet, wincing as fresh pain worked through his head. He rested back against the chuck wagon and breathed in deeply.

'Then it happened during the storm. Thing is, Durant killed Joe and I'm gonna get him for it.'

Only then did Blake Durant stir. He flicked his spent cigarette away and walked slowly down to where Lanny Sowarth stood. For a moment they did no more than stare at each other. Then Durant said:

'Sowarth, don't crowd me anymore. I found the old woman and brought her back here. What happened to your brother I don't know. The way I see it, somebody happened by during the storm, saw the old woman and likely figured to get what she had in her rig. We've passed a dozen drifters on our way here, men on the move, taking what they can get their hands on. Looking at it a little deeper, your brother likely saw this somebody, might have tackled him, and was shot. The only other explanation is that your brother, still smarting at what the old woman said to him, squared his account with her. How he got himself shot I don't know . . . a drifter maybe.'

Lanny Sowarth glared furiously at Durant and shook his head. 'It ain't good enough, Durant. My time will come.'

'Well, it won't come until after we get my cattle to town,' Jay Hurwood put in authoritatively. 'I don't know what happened except that I found Joe on his face in the creek, dead. I didn't even see the old woman. Now look. I've got a buyer lined up in Gabriel. When we get the cattle passed over to him, then we'll put all this into the hands of the Gabriel sheriff. After that I'm washing my hands of the whole sorry business.'

Blake Durant turned away from Lanny Sowarth, but Sowarth had the last word. 'Durant, you remember something, eh? As soon as we reach Gabriel, I'll be coming for you.'

'Suit yourself,' Blake told him, crossing to where Hap Wheeler was doling out the evening meal. The rain had cooled down the country and the wind blowing across each of them was dry. There didn't seem any likelihood of more rain. Taking his meal from Wheeler, Blake settled on his saddle and forked beans and stew together on his plate. Then, without looking at any of them, he started to eat.

'It couldn't have been you, Mr Durant,' Dave Crane said as he came back from ground – hitching his horse for the night.

Hurwood had put Lanny Sowarth on herd guard after they had buried Joe Sowarth. From the time the meal had started, Lanny Sowarth had not spoken a word, but had sat moodily silent, stealing looks at Blake Durant.

Durant studied Crane's young face with no apparent interest. 'It's none of your business, Dave,' he said bluntly.

'Well, when we get to town, I'm gonna make it my business, Mr Durant,' Crane said, respect in his voice. 'I'm gonna front up to the Gabriel lawman, whoever he might be, and say my piece. Hell, I saw everything you did, exceptin' for maybe five minutes or so. And you sure enough didn't have time to get to the creek and back.'

Blake made up a cigarette and stared moodily through the gloom. Lanny Sowarth's threats didn't worry him. But he had no wish to kill the cowhand, but he knew he would have to if Sowarth persisted in crowding him. And the only way to stop that, in Blake Durant's mind, was to solve the riddle of Joe Sowarth's death. He could believe that Joe Sowarth had come across the old crone during the storm and that Joe had lost his temper. But then how and why did Joe collect a bullet?

Blake looked to where Jay Hurwood and Wheeler were sitting quietly. He drew in a ragged breath. There was nobody here apart from himself who would lock horns with Joe Sowarth. And he knew that he hadn't done it. Then who?

He settled back, the puzzle running through his mind, wondering if he had stumbled on the real truth of the business, that of the passing through of a drifter on the lookout for anything he could get his hands on. But then wouldn't he have taken Joe's horse and gun and have gone through his saddle-bags? Almost certainly he would have, unless Hurwood's arrival had forced him to flee.

Blake drew on his cigarette and stared into the darkness. As usual, trouble dogged his trail, trouble he hadn't looked for but which he couldn't step away from. But then there was still the end of the drive to complete and Gabriel was another town. Perhaps when they reached the town, Lanny Sowarth would quieten down some and listen to reason. Perhaps. But Blake doubted it.

He rose, flicked his cigarette away, lifted his saddlebag from the wet ground and walked off into the darkness to find a sleeping place for himself. The matter could rest until morning.

Hap Wheeler couldn't sleep. He lay under his blankets, the words of the old crone running through his mind. What had she said to Durant? Something about trails not always being lonely. He didn't know what the hell she had meant by that, but he conceded that Durant was a loner. In three weeks he had done all the work expected of him; and, as Jay Hurwood had told him, Durant was about the best hand he had put on in many years.

Hap rolled onto his side as the wind whipped through the raised canvas. There was no other sound but that of the wind; the others having long since gone to sleep. He thought about the old woman's talk to him. 'Many suns and many moons but there is still time.' Hap smiled to himself. The old woman could sure count. He felt he had lived a hundred years already, but he doubted that he had much time left. At sixty years of age he was no longer fit to ride like Durant and the Sowarth boys or Dave Crane. He had been pensioned into the seat of a chuck wagon. But he didn't mind. He had at times lived reasonably well, and with Gabriel just ahead of him he would have plenty of time and money to idle along. Sooner or later another outfit like Hurwood's would come through looking for a man of his talents and he'd shift on.

'You there, stay put!'

The snarl of words broke through the night's stillness like a whiplash. Hap Wheeler jerked upright, his hand automatically clamping on his carving knife. He felt sweat build up on his brow as silence settled again and tension took hold of him. What the hell was happening? he asked himself. Durant and Lanny Sowarth again?

'Come into the light slowly.'

Hap licked his lips. The voice came from near the wagon. Hap shifted as silently as he could and peered out from under the flap. He saw the glow from the fire, a man's boots planted wide near the edge of the coals, and then another pair of boots walking towards the others. Hap risked the chance of being seen by drawing the canvas flap back quietly. Looking out, he saw Lanny Sowarth stop before Jay Hurwood.

'What the hell were you up to, Lanny?' Hurwood asked gruffly.

'I came here for a drink.'

Hurwood's brows arched and his eyes clouded. 'You always carry a canteen, don't you, especially when you're on night guard over the herd?'

'Tonight I forgot.'

Hurwood looked past him to the rear of the wagon where Lanny Sowarth had come. 'The water barrel's up front, Lanny. You've filled up enough times to know that.'

'I hadn't got to it yet, Hurwood.'

'You didn't seem in much of a hurry, Lanny. Maybe your thirst wasn't all that bad.'

Hap saw Sowarth's face darken and then twist sourly.

'Do I get the water or not, Hurwood?' he asked. 'Or are you rationing it so close to the town?'

Jay Hurwood still stared at him, but suddenly he put up his gun. He dropped down onto his blanket again, but kept his eyes fixed on Sowarth. As Sowarth drew water from a water barrel and drank thirstily, Hurwood said:

'Make that drink be enough until you're relieved, Lanny.'

Sowarth shrugged, wiped his mouth, glanced at Hap Wheeler and saw the knife in his hand. He gave a short laugh and went off towards his horse, which Hap saw he had left standing a good fifty yards up the clearing.

When Sowarth had stepped into the saddle and made off, Wheeler said, 'What the hell was he really after, Jay?'

Hurwood gave a grunt. 'Maybe a gun, maybe something from your wagon, Hap. No worry. I don't think he'll try it again.' Hurwood turned then, and called out, 'Crane, you've got another half hour, then go and relieve Sowarth. Tell Durant when you come off that he can go through till morning.'

There was no answer from Dave Crane for several minutes. Then he called out, 'Durant might take some finding, Mr Hurwood. He left camp an hour ago.'

Hurwood leaned on an elbow. 'That so?'

'It is, Mr Hurwood. Saddled up and rode out.'

41

'Where'd he head?'

'Towards town.'

Hurwood leaned on his elbow for some time before he fell onto his back again. 'Well, maybe he knows what he's doing,' he said. 'If he isn't back when you've finished your time, wake me up.'

'Will do, Mr Hurwood,' Crane mumbled, and silence fell again.

Hap Wheeler went back into the wagon and stretched out. He had a fair idea what the crafty Sowarth had been up to, and he figured Hurwood had it right. But the part that worried Hap most was this proof that Lanny Sowarth really did have it in for Blake Durant, despite all the evidence to prove Durant's innocence. He wondered where it would end, but he was willing to put a decent slice of his pay dirt on Durant. He'd seen him draw a gun twice and he couldn't remember seeing anybody draw faster.

He lay back and thought a little more about Blake Durant. He had come out of nowhere to join the cattle drive. Since then he had kept completely to himself, doing only what was expected of him. But something about him mystified Hap Wheeler. He put it down to the fast draw and the big black. Nobody who was on the drift had the right to own a fine animal like that, the best Hap had ever seen.

So was Durant really a drifter? Or was he something else? Hap pulled his blanket up to his scrawny neck and closed his eyes. He was tired and restless. Gabriel would look really good to him.

# THREE

# CAREFUL MEN

'Where the hell have you been, Durant?'

Blake Durant stood beside Sundown, cleaning flecks of mud off the stallion's hocks. He looked up at Jay Hurwood through the gray light of sunup.

'Camped out,' Blake said.

'You have a camp here. Hell, you missed the third watch.'

'I figured it better to miss a watch than the rest of the drive, Hurwood. You ready to break camp?'

Hurwood scowled at him, knowing Durant was right, but disliking the way Durant made him feel inferior. In three weeks he hadn't been able to find fault with the man, yet in some peculiar way, Durant

44

annoyed him.

He pushed the thought out of his head and said, 'Let's break camp. I'll have you riding point and Sowarth riding drag. OK?'

Durant shrugged, gave Sundown a pat and swung up. Hap Wheeler, putting out the fire as Durant went past, called out:

'You missed breakfast, Durant. I ain't got time now to start all over.'

'No matter, Hap. You've fed me well for three whole weeks.'

The compliment did nothing to lessen Hap's annoyance with Durant. He liked to see every one of his team well fed. He was used to their grumbling about the monotonous fare, but then he'd never been on a cattle drive when there hadn't been complaints from the men, no matter how much he tried with the little available to him. It was beef and beans, if an outfit travelled twenty miles or ten thousand. Hap figured that the men, usually born to this life, should have given him credit for what he'd tried to do. But none did. But those like Durant, who never made a complaint, really upset him. The bellyaching was at least a break in the monotony.

Durant went on, leaving Hap kicking at the fire. Crane was already coming across the clearing, and Jay Hurwood, on a big roan, was on top of the rise.

Seeing Lanny Sowarth at the rear of the herd, Hurwood gave his signals, then Durant and Crane, riding different sides of the herd, got the cattle moving. Hurwood waited until the cattle went past him, then he dropped in at the rear of the herd with Lanny Sowarth. He didn't bother to look Sowarth's way, nor did he speak to him.

So the herd went on, across the muddy clearing and onto higher ground. In two hours they were across the creek where Joe Sowarth's body had been found and then they reached the wide prairie that led to Gabriel.

Gabriel was a small cattle town that lived on the trail herds. From its railhead, cattle were shipped east and north. The town itself was hardly more than a cluster of buildings surrounding cattle yards. The yards stretched in every direction, each linked by a series of gates and chutes which ended at the railhead platform. From the platform timber walks had been built to transfer the cattle into freight cars. There was one walkway provided for people who wished to travel on the cattle trains, but since only losers and quitters used the warped walkway, it was so narrow that only one person could use it at a time.

In this walkway, Sheriff Rod Plimpton now stood,

right hand to his eyes to shield them from the late afternoon sun. Plimpton watched the cattle heading for their yard. He decided this outfit knew its business, for the cattle came on in a close – packed bunch, without hurry, not a single steer breaking out of the group. He assessed the herd as being close to five hundred head, a big herd by any standards. Roger Thomas from Cheyenne had already bought the herd, but Plimpton and a lot of bored citizens had turned out to witness the arrival of the cattle and men. Roger Thomas was standing only a few yards from the sheriff, looking like a dude in an eastern business suit.

'I guess what Hurwood said is true, Thomas,' Plimpton called out.

'He struck me as an honest cattleman,' Thomas returned, his small, pinched face showing the effects of Gabriel's heat. 'Those cattle are in really good condition.'

'They came through better than the hands, if that feller is an example,' Plimpton said, pointing to Lanny Sowarth, who had just come into sight on the edge of the herd.

'He looks to be the only one the trip's affected,' Roger Thomas said, joining the sheriff now. He suddenly frowned. 'Sheriff, do you notice anything peculiar about all of them?'

Plimpton looked, frowning with concentration. 'Just a tired bunch,' he muttered.

'Not one of them is carrying a gun, Sheriff,' Thomas said. 'I'd expect that a man in your position would have noticed that right off.'

Plimpton looked more intently, swinging his gaze from Durant to Crane and then to Lanny Sowarth. Then Jay Hurwood rode from the head of the herd and came directly towards him.

'All are unarmed but Hurwood,' Plimpton said. 'Now what in all blazes does that mean?'

Thomas shrugged and went down to the platform's end to meet Hurwood. Plimpton, after scrubbing the back of his grimy neck, followed him. When Hurwood drew up, smiling, Thomas extended his hand. 'I don't think there will be any difficulties, Mr Hurwood. You can yard them and then we'll do a count.'

'That'll be organized in about twenty minutes from now, Thomas. Your part of the deal will be OK, eh?'

Thomas returned Hurwood's smile. 'The money is awaiting you in the bank, Mr Hurwood. They're a fine bunch of steers, just as you said.'

Hurwood nodded. 'We nursed them good and the pastures were the best I've gone through for years. It just could be that I'll be returning to

Dorrigo and getting myself another bunch. With the men I've got now, I can do three, four trips a year.'

'A lot of hungry people will be indebted to you,' Thomas said.

But Rod Plimpton, suddenly impatient with the small talk, pushed forward and gained Hurwood's attention by his surly and concentrated stare. 'Your men aren't wearing guns, Hurwood. Is there a reason for that?'

'There is,' Hurwood said.

Plimpton licked his dry lips and waited for him to go on. When Jay Hurwood showed no intention of doing this, he growled, 'Well, damn you, what is it? Is that bunch kill – crazy, maybe?'

Hurwood shrugged and looked at Lanny Sowarth who was closing his flank towards the first of the long cattle yards. Durant and Crane had closed up the other side, and Hap Wheeler, whose chuck wagon had served to push the back of the herd along with its rattling noise, had begun to sweep away from the cattle and head into the main street of Gabriel.

Hurwood said, 'There was a little trouble, Sheriff Plimpton, which I will tell you about later, just as soon as I get those cattle freighted onto the train and get my money.'

'You'll tell me now, damn you!' Plimpton growled, pushing Thomas roughly aside and glaring at Hurwood. 'I've got a clean, quiet town and I ain't standin' for any gun – crazy jaspers tearin' it up when you take the reins off them. I want to know about this outfit, Hurwood, and by hell you're gonna tell me.'

Hurwood looked at Thomas, who had moved away because he hated being dwarfed by big men like Plimpton, and also because he didn't like the stench of sweat coming from the big man.

'There's been a killing,' Hurwood said tonelessly. 'But take my word for it, Plimpton, I checked the matter out fully and there's nothing anybody can do about it.'

'A man from your outfit?' Plimpton asked tightly. 'Have they been tearin' at each other, which is the reason why you took their guns?'

Hurwood nodded. 'It was one of my men. It happened during the storm that hit us late yesterday evening. I returned to the camp and found him dead.'

'Shot?'

Hurwood nodded grimly. 'Yes.'

'Then somebody fired the shot, mister,' Plimpton said. His eyes were gleaming now and sweat glistened on his fat face. 'Who?'

Hurwood shook his head. 'Nobody knows.'

Plimpton's mouth gaped. 'You've got an outfit, then one gets killed and nobody knows anything about it?'

'That's right, Sheriff. I just told you – it happened during the storm that hit our camp. Everybody was working hard to stop the herd from stampeding, so nobody saw much of what the others were doing. When the storm stopped, Joe Sowarth was dead.'

Plimpton frowned at him. 'Who the hell is Sowarth? Where's he from? Is he a trouble – maker?'

Hurwood raked a hand through his hair and looked impatiently at Roger Thomas again. 'He was just a hired hand. There was a storm, and after it was over I found him lying in a creek, face down, with a bullet in him. Naturally I got the men together, but none of them could solve the problem of who killed Sowarth. As for taking the men's guns, I did that because there's bad blood between Sowarth's brother and one of the other men.'

Plimpton's eyes flashed and he shifted closer. By then Durant and Crane had begun to steer the cattle into the bottom yards, while Wheeler had entered the main street and was hitching the chuck wagon to a line pole. Lanny Sowarth was sitting his horse, a hundred feet from Crane and Durant, his stare fixed on them.

'So now we're getting some place, Hurwood,' Plimpton said. 'The dead man has a brother and he claims another of your men killed him. Right?'

'Something like that.'

'Well, you can forget about getting these cattle any further, Hurwood. Just bring your men to the jailhouse. I'll take it from there.'

'The hell I will, Plimpton,' growled Hurwood. 'I've come hundreds of miles and I nursed these steers every mile of the way. I'm not gonna let them stray now.'

Plimpton opened his mouth to argue further, but Roger Thomas said quietly, 'Sheriff, be sensible about it. What will another fifteen minutes or so matter? Those men don't look as though they're going anywhere; and Hurwood's shown good sense in disarming them. Actually, Sheriff Plimpton, I'm going to insist that you postpone your investigation until my cattle are loaded onto the train.'

'Insist?' Plimpton barked at him. 'By hell – '

'As a visitor to your town who intends to come here a great many times in the future, to use your railroad, your saloon and your rooming house, and who will in time set up an office here, I think I have that right. I don't think too many of your towns-people will approve of your letting a man lose time and money, because of a selfish whim.'

Plimpton gaped at him. Hurwood turned his horse slightly and the movement brought Plimpton's stare his way again. But when Plimpton saw that Hurwood was making no attempt to take matters into his own hands, he took his gaze from him and studied the cowhands who had most of the herd in the bottom yards.

'OK, then. What do a few minutes matter? But so help me, Hurwood, just as soon as this business is finished I want all of your outfit in my office. And they don't get their guns back until I've talked to them. You got that?'

Hurwood nodded and hurried off. Roger Thomas settled over the platform rail and watched the work going on below.

'A real good bunch,' Thomas muttered, but his attempt to ease the tension between himself and Plimpton earned only a grunt from Plimpton. The big lawman strode down the platform to the walkway. Then he headed uptown.

Sheriff Rod Plimpton had plenty of time to prepare himself for the arrival of the Hurwood crew. He was seated behind his desk, his gun on the desk close to his right hand. The rest of the office was completely bare, which was deliberate. Plimpton liked visitors to feel naked.

As Hurwood came in, followed by an old – timer with bushy whiskers and then by a young cowhand, Plimpton signaled for them to line up against the wall. Hap Wheeler, scowling, made no move to follow his directions, but said, 'You gonna inspect our brands, Sheriff?'

Plimpton's mouth tightened. 'Just do like you're told, old man, and pronto.'

Blake Durant stepped into the room. Plimpton switched his gaze to him and was taken by the wide shoulders and easy movement of the man. He was also impressed by Durant's confident, unwavering gaze. Durant was walking to join Crane and Hurwood when Lanny Sowarth entered the jail-house office. Plimpton's expression darkened. Sowarth looked sourly at him, then glanced at Blake Durant before he crossed the room.

Plimpton, about to order him to line up with the others, noticed that Sowarth's gaze remained fixed on Durant. The deep – seated hatred in the cowhand's eyes told Plimpton that these were the two Hurwood had mentioned.

'OK, Hurwood, let's have the full story,' Plimpton said. He sat back, hands folded, his hat on the back of his head.

'I've told you what I know,' Hurwood said shortly.

'Well, tell it again, mister. Nobody's leaving this office until I get to the bottom of this killing.'

'Two killings,' put in Hap Wheeler. Plimpton's body stiffened and he came forward with a jerk. His big hand slammed down on the desk. 'Two?'

Hap nodded. 'I figured a smart man like you would have all the facts by now, Sheriff.'

Plimpton scowled blackly at him. He knew Wheeler's kind, hard to handle, using their age to protect themselves. Plimpton came slowly to his feet and leaned across the desk, supporting his huge weight on his fists. His look swung to each in turn.

'Now get this. I want the full story from Hurwood – and nobody else interrupts. If there were two killings I want to know all about 'em. No lies now, and no covering up. Just the straight truth.'

Jay Hurwood looked calmly back at him and said, 'I can only tell you as much as I know, Plimpton. An old woman drove a rig into our camp just before a storm broke. It seems she made something of a nuisance of herself and – '

'She wasn't doing anybody any harm, Mr Hurwood,' put in Dave Crane. 'Hell, all she did was read our hands and tell what she saw there.'

'OK, OK,' Hurwood said impatiently. 'She didn't do anybody any harm, but some of you said she upset Joe Sowarth.'

'Called him a bad 'un,' Wheeler offered. 'And Joe sure enough didn't like it. He went for her and Durant here stopped him. Joe tried to hammer Durant down, but he came off second best and then he went for his gun. But he didn't win any notches doing that either. Then Lanny over there bought in and was also stopped in his tracks by Durant. Then the storm hit us.'

Plimpton was clearly becoming confused. But before he could demand anything further Hurwood told Hap to go on. Wheeler was only too eager to keep the spotlight.

'Well, it seems that during the storm somebody shot the old woman. When the storm'd gone, Durant, looking for strays, found her body and brought it back to camp. We buried her and were waiting for Hurwood to show up, nobody having seen Joe Sowarth for some time. Then Hurwood came with Joe's body slung over his horse.'

Plimpton came around his desk, scowling. 'So who killed the old woman?'

Hap, who had assumed the role of chief speaker, shook his head. 'We don't know. The rain washed out all tracks leading away from her busted rig. There just wasn't anything to go on.'

Plimpton raked his hair and settled back on the desk's edge. He breathed in a deep sigh. 'Then who killed this Joe Sowarth?'

'Durant.' This from Lanny Sowarth.

Plimpton swung about, staring intently at Lanny. 'That so, mister?'

'Sure. He was scared. Joe said he'd settle with Durant when we got here to town. He used the storm as cover and killed my brother. And for that I'm gonna settle with him.'

Plimpton straightened and studied each of the four men against the wall. Finally his gaze on Durant, he said, 'You're Durant?'

Blake nodded.

'What've you got to say for yourself, eh? This man's made an accusation against you.'

'I didn't kill his brother,' was Durant's cool reply.

'But you were scared of him, like he just said?'

Blake shook his head. 'Joe Sowarth didn't worry me in the least.'

'You're a damn liar, Durant!' Lanny said, stepping away from the wall, fists clenched and hatred burning in his black eyes.

Plimpton reached back, picked up his gun from the desk and leveled it on Lanny. 'Mister, we're just talkin' at the moment. Nothin' else. You settle back now.'

'Go fry,' Lanny snapped back at him.

Plimpton's face flushed with anger. Lanny defied

his fiery look for a moment and then slumped back to the wall and continued to glare at Blake Durant.

Plimpton said, 'Well, we've got two different stories. Who else has something to say?'

'Me,' said Dave Crane, remembering his promise to Durant to speak his mind when they hit town. Plimpton nodded for him to proceed and Crane said, 'Joe Sowarth's body was found at a creek four or five miles from camp. I was with Durant during the storm, every minute of it. When the storm lifted he said to me to stay with the cattle and he went off to look for strays. It was only five minutes or so when he returned with the old woman's body and I joined him on the ride back to camp, where Hap was. Lanny Sowarth over there arrived not long after. We all went back and searched the valley where Durant had found the old woman, but there was no tracks. So we came back to camp to bury the old woman and wait.'

'Which, in a nutshell, Sheriff Plimpton,' Hurwood said, 'clears Durant of Joe Sowarth's murder.'

'Why does it?' asked Plimpton.

'Because, on Crane's say – so, Durant wasn't out of his sight for more than five minutes. He could not have ridden to the creek where I found Joe's body and got back to camp in time. It just wasn't possible.'

'Crane got his times mixed up,' Lanny Sowarth said. 'And I'll get him for that.'

'You can go to blazes, Sowarth,' Crane barked back. 'I'm not scared of you. You didn't look so damned good when you and your brother tackled Durant. He put paid to both of you as easy as blinking.'

Lanny Sowarth's face went tight with bitterness. His lips curled back in a savage snarl and Plimpton measured him with another warning look and a wave of his gun. Lanny stood there, glaring at Crane and Blake Durant.

'So there you have it, Plimpton,' Hurwood said with finality. 'It's a dead end as I see it. There's no clue to who killed the old woman. There's also no clue to who killed Joe Sowarth. So what the hell do you aim to do about it? Keep us here all damn night? These men and I have some business to transact, then I'm washing my hands of the whole business. I don't like trouble, and worse, I don't like mysteries. For mine, these men, when I pay them off, can have their guns back and do what they like.'

Plimpton looked uncomfortable. His face told the story of his complete inability to understand this business. 'Two people were killed in my territory,' he muttered.

'Outside it, Sheriff,' Hurwood said and moved

away from the wall.

'In or out, it doesn't make any difference.'

Hurwood smiled thinly at him. 'Sheriff, there are no tracks out there, and nobody here can make head nor tail of what happened. So how could you, experienced lawman or not, ride out and discover what we couldn't? No – the business is finished with as far as I'm concerned, and I advise you to think likewise.'

Plimpton licked his lips and fingered sweat from his brow. He continued to look at the others. Hap Wheeler broke the silence by saying:

'Hurwood, I'll be in the saloon when you want to pay me off. And don't be too long because I've got enough money for maybe three drinks only. Come on, Crane, there ain't nothin' more anybody can do here.'

Dave Crane looked defiantly at Plimpton. The sheriff motioned for the pair of them to go, and he made no attempt to stop Hurwood following them. But when Blake Durant and Lanny Sowarth came away from the wall, Plimpton said:

'No. You pair wait awhile.'

Lanny Sowarth swung back, glaring at Plimpton. 'What now, damn you?'

'Now you listen, mister,' Plimpton said angrily. 'I got the impression from that heap of gum wash I just heard that you two are gonna gun for each other. Well, that ain't gonna happen in my town, you hear? If you even as much as cuss each other, I'm gonna throw you both in a cell. OK, Durant, you move out first and keep going.'

Durant looked coolly at Lanny Sowarth and walked to the doorway. He hesitated there, as if about to turn back to give some parting advice to Lanny, but then, with a shrug of his shoulders, he stepped out to the boardwalk.

Above the sound of Durant's footsteps, Plimpton said tightly, 'Sowarth, you hear me good now. By the look of that jasper, he ain't gonna be easy for any man to handle, and what the kid said sorta backs that up, doesn't it? So you forget about your brother, get drunk and mind your manners. If you don't so help me, what I said before goes – you'll spend all your time in my town in one of the cells back there.'

Lanny drew himself tall and wiped his hands down his levis. Then he went to the doorway, turned his head and fixed Rod Plimpton with a baleful look. 'If you know what's good for you, Sheriff, you'll keep out of this. There ain't no law that says a man can't go after his brother's killer.'

'By hell, in this town, mister—'

Lanny cut him off. 'In this or any other town,

61

Sheriff, I do as I damned well like. If you don't believe that, you get on the telegraph and check through Dorrigo, Beaver Creek and Temple Ridge. You'll see I'm known well enough.'

Plimpton scowled at him. 'How damn well, Sowarth?'

Lanny smiled. 'Better'n most. Durant hasn't got a dog's chance, but it won't be a cold killing. I don't have to resort to that, so you stir up your buryin' man.'

'For the last time, Sowarth,' Plimpton said angrily, moving from the front of the desk, his gun still in his hand, 'this is my town and I intend to . . .' He cut himself off when Lanny walked out.

Plimpton hurried across the room, bad – tempered because he felt he'd made a fool of himself. He strode onto the boardwalk. Lanny Sowarth was already crossing the street where Hurwood was returning their guns to Crane and Hap Wheeler. Plimpton swore under his breath. He couldn't prevent Hurwood from returning the guns for there was no ordinance in town against the carrying of weapons. Then he saw Lanny Sowarth stop before Hurwood and get his gun. Lanny checked the gun carefully, then wheeled about and studied the street.

Plimpton leaned against a building wall, cursing

under his breath. What the hell could he do? He couldn't follow the pair about waiting for them to let off sparks. He would just have to bide his time and try to be on hand when the shooting started. And from the look of Lanny Sowarth, it wouldn't be long in coming.

# FOUR

## 'BE TOLD!'

Blake Durant left the main street with Sundown
trailing him on a slack rein. He entered the mouth
of the livery stable laneway and walked down it. As
always his first concern after a long, hard ride was to
see to Sundown. Later he would indulge himself.
The thought of a drink, with town talk washing
about him, appealed to him mightily just then. But
he doubted if he would be able to find the time to
enjoy such relaxation that evening, not with Lanny
Sowarth on the prod. Thinking about him, as he
had from the moment he had left the jailhouse,
Blake wondered if it might not be best to get Lanny
on his own and try to talk some sense into him.

Even if that failed, he would at least have the advantage of having Lanny Sowarth where he could watch him. The other way, letting Sowarth come for him, didn't appeal to Blake at all.

Reaching the stables, he called the attendant out and spent several minutes talking to him while Sundown became accustomed to the stranger's smell and the feel of the man's hands. Blake explained that the horse, after being introduced, would give him no trouble, but he warned him not to let anybody else near the horse for fear Sundown would get fidgety.

He was watching the attendant lead Sundown off when Dave Crane called to him. Durant turned and saw the young cowboy hurrying towards him, one gun in his holster and Blake's Colt in his hand. Blake took his gun, checked it, then pushed it into his holster.

'Hap and I were just talking,' Crane said. 'We reckoned you'd best stay with us at least until we get paid off by Hurwood. Hap figures, and I go along with him, that Sowarth won't risk doing anything loco while we're in a bunch.'

Blake looked easily past Crane and shook his head. 'You and Hap have worked hard on the drive. You deserve a trouble free time, so go have it. Don't worry about me.'

'But Hap says – and I agree with him – that Sowarth ain't the gun – slouch his brother Joe was. We've been riding with Lanny for several months now and though he wasn't as sour – tempered as Joe, and Joe did most of the talking, at times Lanny just naturally decided things for them. And Joe never argued back. When something really important happened, it was Lanny who did the thinking for both of them. We figure that means something.'

Blake gave Crane a thin smile and placed a hand on his broad shoulder. 'Dave, you'll make it in this country if you mind your own business. I'm not telling you to get to hell out of my hair, but I'm asking you to leave me be. If Lanny wants to go on with this, he'll regret it.'

Dave Crane studied Blake intently for some time before he suddenly nodded his head. 'Hell, I know that and Hap says it, too. You can take a dozen like him. But Hap figures Lanny might know that too, and it'll be something different than man against man.'

'Whatever it is, I'll be ready for him,' Blake said, then he turned away and leaned across the horse yard rail to watch Sundown check out his new surroundings. He heard Dave Crane leave and was relieved the young man had taken his advice. The one thing he didn't want was having to worry about old Hap and young Dave if Lanny Sowarth went berserk. Sundown stood with head lifted, his stare sweeping across the heads of the other horses in the yard. Blake Durant noticed that every one of the horses stood stiffly now, as if uncertain about the big black stallion.

Smiling, Blake turned away from the rails but had gone only two steps when a shout from his right brought him whirling about. His hand went immediately to his gun butt as his stare probed the gloom at the laneway's end. He saw Dave Crane's tall slim figure coming his way.

'Durant, watch out! Sowarth's there!'

A gunshot broke through the words and Blake felt the burn of a bullet along his forearm. His heels dug into the ground as his weight went back on them. Then his gun exploded and the shot went into the middle of the laneway mouth to slam into a figure crouched there.

A cry came from out of the gloom and then Dave Crane stopped running and turned, his gun leveled, covering the lane – way mouth. Blake Durant walked slowly forward, his eyes becoming quickly accustomed to the gloom. He saw a figure kneeling on the ground, hands sweeping out over the surface of the dust as if searching for something. Blake hurried forward and saw Sowarth's gun lying against the wall of the store. He picked it up as Sowarth's pain – tortured, hate – filled eyes blazed at him.

Blake emptied the gun and hurled it over Sowarth's head in the direction of the street.

'Get up!' he said.

Lanny Sowarth remained on his side. Dave Crane joined Blake now and said fiercely, 'Sowarth, you tried to kill Mr Durant cold!'

Sowarth sneered at him. Then he worked his feet up under him and pushed himself against the store wall. A groan came out of him. Blake pulled him upright and slammed him back against the wall just as Sheriff Plimpton came running in from the main street. Plimpton halted a few yards away and demanded:

'What the hell goes on here?'

Dave Crane nodded at Lanny Sowarth. 'He tried to gun down Mr Durant, Sheriff. Tried to do it cold.'

Sowarth looked bitterly at Dave Crane and pushed at Durant. As Durant moved away from Sowarth, Plimpton saw Sowarth's bloodied shoulder.

'Mister, I told you in the jailhouse—'

'Go bury yourself, lawman,' Lanny Sowarth growled back. 'This hasn't got anything to do with you.'

'Any shooting in my town, mister, has plenty to do with me. First we'll get you to the sawbones, then the three of you can come with me to the jailhouse. If I don't get satisfactory talk from all of you, I'll have full cells for the night.'

Lanny Sowarth sniggered and then growled out, 'On what damned charge, lawman?'

'On the charge of attempted murder, Sowarth,' put in Dave Crane. 'I saw you waiting for Mr Durant to come back from the stables. Earlier I saw you get your gun from Hurwood and I knew by the look of you that you were up to no good. You're scum, Sowarth, right through.'

Lanny Sowarth's left arm shot out and clamped on Crane's windpipe. But Blake Durant slapped Sowarth's hand away and slammed him back against the wall. Sheriff Plimpton then shouldered his way between them, pushing Durant off. He showed his gun in the space between them and snarled:

'Now see here, the bunch of you. This is the end of it, do you hear? One more bit of trouble and by hell it'll go bad for all of you.'

'Stinkin' scum,' grated Dave Crane, but Blake Durant merely stood back, his face clouded and his eyes fixed on Lanny Sowarth.

'Sowarth, hear me out,' Durant muttered. 'I didn't kill your brother and I hold nothing against

69

you for this bullet graze you gave me. But next time you come for me, I'll kill you.'

Plimpton studied Blake coolly for a time before he said, 'Maybe you don't hold anything against him, Durant, but I sure enough do.'

'I'm laying no charges,' Blake said. Then, as Dave Crane was about to speak, Blake shook his head at him. 'Keep out of it, Dave.'

'You mean you're not gonna have me hold him for attempted murder, Durant?' Plimpton said angrily.

'Coming against me was more like committing suicide,' Blake said. 'Anyhow, by the look of that shoulder he won't be worrying about anything but pain for some time. Let's leave it at that.'

As Blake spoke, Jay Hurwood came hurrying into the top of the laneway. A crowd had gathered and Hurwood forced his way through, holding a number of bulky envelopes in his left hand. Hurwood had cleaned himself and changed his clothes and looked every inch a prosperous businessman.

'What the hell's going on?' he asked gruffly. 'You men causing trouble again?'

'If you'd held onto those guns a while longer, Hurwood, maybe there wouldn't have been trouble,' Plimpton said. 'By hell, you've brought a real curly outfit into my town, mister, and I'm not about to forget it.'

Hurwood looked blandly at Plimpton. 'Sheriff, I'm not responsible for the actions of my men in town. On the range, yes, but not here. Now I'm about to pay 'em off.' He showed the bulky envelopes and then looked at Lanny Sowarth. If he saw the bloodied shoulder, he made no mention of it. He tossed one of the envelopes to Sowarth, then handed others to Durant and Dave Crane and said, 'When I pay off Wheeler, I'm out of this, Plimpton. I don't intend to sign on trouble – makers for any trip I make in the future, so these men can do what they like. I'm through with them. I wash my hands of the whole business.'

Plimpton scowled at Hurwood, who was turning to leave when a woman's voice sounded from the back of the crowd at the laneway's mouth.

'Jay!'

Lanny Sowarth moved along the wall, clutching his right shoulder. Rod Plimpton, uncertain about how much authority he had over these newcomers to his town, scowled after Sowarth for a moment, then motioned for Durant and Crane to proceed in front of him. Hurwood in the meantime had hurried to the edge of the crowd and drawn a tall woman to one side of the boardwalk. Blake Durant got a glimpse of her face before she went into the gloom of the overhang. She was a fine looking woman of about thirty, with short – cropped dark hair contrasting with her white blouse and skirt.

He took no more interest in her as the crowd parted to let him go through after Lanny Sowarth, who picked up his empty gun from the dust where Durant had thrown it, and after a sullen glance at Durant, walked off. Plimpton watched him go, laying a hand on Durant's shoulder.

'I'm not finished with you yet, Durant. You either, Crane.'

Crane stopped beside Durant as Plimpton dispersed the crowd with blunt orders. Plimpton then stood and mopped sweat from his brow. Hurwood and the young woman were still waiting on the boardwalk's edge, Hurwood with a hand supporting her elbow. But it was plain to Blake Durant when he caught her gaze that the woman was in no hurry to move off. In fact, her gaze steadied on him and he saw a gleam of interest enter her eyes. At closer range, he saw that her skin was velvet smooth and that her tall body was lushly shaped.

Hurwood tried to turn her away but she shrugged out of his grip and continued to study Blake Durant. 'Are these your men, Jay?' she asked.

Hurwood frowned at her. 'They were, Merle, but

not any longer. I've paid them off.'

'Then you're not making any more trips, Jay?'

Hurwood's frown deepened and it was clear he wanted to shift on and didn't much like answering her questions. 'Not with them, I'm not.'

'But you said they were the best outfit you'd ever had. What's made you change your mind?'

Hurwood was now openly impatient with her. He took her elbow again and steered her a few steps away. But she stopped again, sweeping her hair back so that her blouse tightened across her bosom. Hurwood stood glaring at her and she ignored him.

Plimpton took Durant's attention from the woman by saying, 'What the hell do you intend to do now?'

Blake shrugged. 'It's up to Sowarth, isn't it?'

'Maybe some of it is. But you're involved up to your teeth, mister, and I'm gonna help you get uninvolved. Maybe you should saddle up and ride out. You've been paid off and there ain't nothing but trouble in this town for you. You do that and I'll see that Sowarth stays about for a time. If he follows you finally, you should have enough start on him to dodge him.'

Blake smiled thinly. 'I've just ridden a lot of miles, Sheriff, and I was looking forward to the hospitality of your town. When I'm good and ready I'll move on, but nobody like Sowarth is going to force me to do so before then.'

Blake eased the big man aside and glanced at Dave Crane, who said, 'I'm for moving on, Durant. Hell, we can find another town real easy. Sowarth's mean and since he's hurt now and made one mistake, he won't be quick to make another.'

'Let's have a drink,' Blake told him, then he walked past the scowling Rod Plimpton. He heard the woman speak but he ignored her. Then he heard footsteps going the other way. He was mildly curious about the woman, since in all the weeks in Hurwood's company he hadn't heard the man mention a woman. It was plain that he owned her, or at least thought he did. Dave Crane ranged up beside Durant and after a quick glance at his sober face, walked silently beside him.

They turned into the saloon and found it noisy and packed. Blake found a place at the bar counter for them and ordered drinks. He looked about but there was no sign of Hap Wheeler. They had two drinks before Jay Hurwood entered the saloon and, seeing them, came down the bar. He dropped an envelope onto the counter and asked, 'Where's Wheeler?'

'Was here earlier,' Crane told him. 'Soon as we left the jailhouse he came in here while I took

Durant's gun to him.' Crane looked about him and finally located Hap Wheeler seated at a table at the far end of the room with three old – timers. They had a bottle of whiskey in front of them and Hap looked to be in fine spirits. Then he sighted Durant, Crane and Hurwood and waved vigorously. Blake Durant took his glass and led the way to Hap, but before he reached the table Hurwood pushed in front of him and tossed the envelope onto the table.

'Paid in full, Wheeler,' Hurwood said.

Hap looked up keenly at him. 'You sound like that was tearing a slice out of your heart, Hurwood. Hell, you don't mind payin', do you, after the good trip you had?'

Hurwood looked uncomfortably down at him and shook his head. 'No, I'm glad to pay up, Wheeler. All of you worked well.'

'So sit and have a drink with us and meet some of my friends. Hell, all that time on the trail, living together, a man can't just pay up and run off.'

'I've . . . I've got some business to do first, Wheeler,' Hurwood excused himself. 'Later maybe.'

'Suit yourself,' Wheeler said, looking disappointed. Then Hurwood stepped away from the table and Hap invited Crane and Blake Durant to sit down.

Filling his glass from Hap Wheeler's bottle,

Crane said, 'There was trouble with Sowarth.'

Wheeler's eyebrows rose and his jaw came up. 'That so?'

Crane nodded. 'He took a shot at Durant. Luckily for Durant, the shot only grazed his forearm. But Durant put a slug into Sowarth's shoulder. I reckon he'll be laid up for a few days at least, maybe a week.'

'Good enough,' Hap Wheeler said, filling Durant's glass. He then picked up the envelope and stuffed it in his pocket. 'Wonder who gets Joe Sowarth's pay dirt?' he said.

Crane frowned. 'Guess that's Hurwood's business, Hap. And Lanny's. Who are your friends?'

Hap Wheeler introduced the three old – timers who seemed interested in nothing but the whiskey. Grunts greeted Crane and Durant's acknowledgement of Wheeler's introductions. Durant then filled the other glasses, and turning in his chair looked about the room. It felt good to be in a saloon, with a drink before him and time on his hands. It kept loneliness from crowding in on him, although he knew that later it would come back, torturing him with memories of the past, memories which had faded a little but didn't appear likely to ever disappear.

The noise went on about them and Crane and

Hap Wheeler began to discuss plans for the future. Blake Durant withdrew into himself, ignoring the talk so that after a time Wheeler and Crane became quiet too. The three old – timers, having got a bottle of whiskey from Wheeler, went on their way and Wheeler, leaning forward said:

'Crane tells me Hurwood's got himself a woman. He sure works fast, don't he?'

'She was waiting for him,' Blake said.

Wheeler looked surprised. 'Now how in hell would you know that, Durant? You never knew Hurwood until you linked up with us out on the trail, did you?'

'I know something about women, Hap,' Durant told him. 'She looks to me like a woman who's owned.'

'She looked damn pretty to me,' put in Dave Crane. 'Hell, what I wouldn't give to get my hands on somebody like her!'

'You wouldn't know what the hell to do with her,' Wheeler teased, getting a grin from Durant.

From that point, Blake Durant brightened up a little. It wasn't until one of the saloon girls approached Crane that he rose and excused himself. He ignored Crane when asked where he was going, then he picked up his change and walked the length of the saloon. At the batwings, he stepped aside to let Sheriff Plimpton come through, and he would have gone on if Plimpton hadn't said:

'You don't drink with lawmen, Durant?'

Blake grinned at him. 'I don't mind, Sheriff.'

'I'm invitin' you to.'

Blake nodded and crossed to the bar with Plimpton, who put some money on the counter and stared thoughtfully down at his hands for a time. Then, 'This whole business worries me, Durant. Two dead out there on the range and nobody knows anything about it. Something smells in this.'

Blake agreed with him. On the way to town and during his brief stay, he'd done a lot of wondering himself, but hadn't come up with any answers. Accepting his drink which Plimpton passed across to him, he sipped it before saying, 'I don't suppose you know of any late arrival in town last night, Sheriff? Somebody soaked to the skin, who'd maybe come through mud country?'

Plimpton shook his head. 'I checked about – at the stables, the rooming house and the Cowboys' Rest. Nobody looking for a bath or a bed came in last night or early this morning. In a town this size, strangers don't go unnoticed.'

'The killer might have doubled back on his tracks,' Blake suggested.

Plimpton nodded. 'Might have, if he figured

three or four days' ride the other way was better than spending some time in my town.'

Blake finished his drink and ordered another. He was conscious that Plimpton was regarding him curiously, clearly unable to make him out. So he said, 'Sheriff, I linked up with Hurwood's outfit three weeks ago. I was riding up from Temple Creek, on the drift, and it suited me to have a little company for a time.'

Plimpton straightened, frowning. 'That's what you are then, Durant – a drifter?'

'I move about.'

Plimpton's gaze went up and down Blake's work – trimmed body. 'You don't look like an ordinary drifter to me, Durant. And I just saw your black stallion. Hell, he'd cost a man half a year's pay dirt.'

'I've had him for quite awhile,' Blake said.

'Saddle's real fancy too, Durant, and those clothes you're wearing – they didn't come off no scarecrow.'

Blake smiled. 'A man on the drift doesn't have to be down on his luck, Sheriff. Let's leave it at that, eh?'

Plimpton sighed and then shrugged. 'OK, I guess a man only gets the answers another man wants to give him. Do you intend staying and letting Sowarth come after you?'

'I haven't decided.'

'Be a help to me if you moved on.'

Blake shook his head. 'I didn't lurk in a corner and fire a shot, Sheriff. You go check out the other man. He's the one who'll cause trouble, not me.'

Plimpton finished his drink and looked about the saloon until he sighted Crane and Hap Wheeler and the bar girl, who was now sitting with them. Plimpton ran a hand through his hair, replaced his hat and without another word went off in their direction.

Blake Durant picked up his change and left the saloon. He stopped outside momentarily, his stare sweeping the opposite boardwalk. Then, seeing nothing to worry him, he turned to the right and headed for the rooming house.

Entering it minutes later, he found Hurwood's woman sitting at a window, impatiently drumming her fingers on a table top. When she saw Blake, she leaned back, smiling. Blake nodded in her direction and headed for the foyer desk where a bald – headed clerk was fingering through a magazine. Blake reached past him and turned the room ledger towards himself and picked up a pen. The clerk looked up then, studied him briefly, checked Blake's signature and then, turning, pulled a key from a nail behind him. Handing it to Blake, he muttered, 'Top of the stairs, Mr Durant.'

Blake thanked him and was turning away when Hurwood's woman appeared at his elbow. 'You're retiring so soon?' she asked.

Blake held her look and nodded. 'Been a long trip.'

'I'm Merle Butler,' she said.

Blake nodded and then started to move away again. But she put a hand on his forearm and Blake was surprised at the coldness of her fingers. 'Jay's left me alone for half an hour now. Couldn't you sit with me until he gets back? I'm nervous, the way men come in and stare at me.'

'Where's he gone?' Blake asked.

'To check on the loading of the cattle onto the train,' she said. 'Now why would a man who's driven a herd of cattle such a long distance want a last look at them? You'd think he'd be happy just to sell them and make his profit, wouldn't you?'

Blake shrugged. He found Merle Butler to be extremely attractive, but the way she looked so directly at him and was so familiar with him worried him a little. Since the death of Louise Yerby he had known quite a number of women, and had usually felt comfortable with them. But Merle appeared to be demanding something of him.

He said, 'What Hurwood does is no concern of

mine, Miss Butler. But don't worry about sitting alone here. This is a peaceful town and it's run right. Nobody will bother you.'

Merle looked disappointed. 'You don't like Jay, do you, Mr Durant?'

Blake was surprised that she knew his name. 'I don't think of Hurwood one way or another, Miss Butler,' he answered. 'Now, if you'll excuse me, I have things to do . . . get settled and the like. Maybe we'll meet another time.'

'There might not be another time,' she was quick to reply. 'Jay is terribly jealous. He hardly lets me out of his sight.'

Blake thought of the three months Hurwood had been on the trail, unable to check on her movements. He vaguely wondered what she had done in that time. He said, 'I'm really very tired.'

Merle's eyes mirrored her annoyance and her lips curled a little. 'Very well then, Mr Durant. If you're frightened of Jay, I suppose I can't blame you. I was merely trying to be friendly and since Jay has already told me that you're a lonely, withdrawn man, I guess I shouldn't have bothered.'

Merle turned away. Blake had a reply on his lips but thought better of it. He went up the stairs, aware that the clerk had no longer any interest in the magazine before him but was following the woman's movements eagerly. By the time Blake reached the top of the stairs, the clerk was already crossing the foyer towards Merle Butler. Blake smiled to himself. One man's medicine, another man's poison.

He found his room, entered and kicked off his boots to stretch out on the bed. The sounds of the town drifted in through the open window. He closed his eyes and then his mind tacked back through time to another place and the woman he had known there. And loved. The pain of her death was still strong in him, and sleep was long in coming . . .

# FIVE

# THE WAITING

Lanny Sowarth pushed himself into a sitting position on the couch and then fell back against the porch wall, heavy sweat beading his brow. He shut his eyes against the drive of pain his movements had awakened in his bandaged shoulder. His breathing was fast and his face was drawn and gray. His lips were almost colorless.

Sitting there on the porch of the doctor's house, Lanny finally relaxed and opened his eyes. He looked out at the town in which he didn't have a single friend. He thought of Durant, the man he was going to kill. Durant had murdered his brother Joe, no matter what everybody else said. Lanny had never relied upon evidence to settle anything. A man hated, he hunted and he killed. That was the beginning and the end of it for him.

He pulled his gun from under the couch pillow with his left hand, studied it a moment, then transferred the gun to his right hand. He held it in his palm while fresh sweat broke out on his sallow – skinned face. His eyes glittering, he closed his fingers slowly over the butt of the gun. A grunt came from him as new waves of pain shot through his shoulder. But he kept at it, working his fingers until he could swing the gun from side to side. A gleam of triumph came into his eyes. Then the door opened and a tall gaunt man in black coat and striped trousers came out, frowning at Lanny.

'If you keep at that, mister, that wound will continue to open and bleed and it'll never heal.'

Lanny stared sourly at him. 'You did your bit, Doc, and you got paid for it – so shut down on the advice, eh?'

Doc Fogarty came across the porch. He settled against the rail and studied Lanny for a time before he spoke again.

'The bullet that smashed your shoulder did as good a job of maiming a man as I've seen in some time. Not only did it tear a lot of flesh and gouge out a large hole, but it splintered the shoulder bone. For the wound to heal you'll have to keep that sling on all the time, get as much rest as you can, and do absolutely nothing with that right hand. Do you understand what I'm trying to tell you?'

Lanny scowled back at him. 'It's my arm, damn you!'

'I know it is, and I'm grateful it's your arm and not mine, Mr Sowarth, believe you me. It will give pain for several weeks, and if you don't follow my advice I'm afraid you'll be permanently crippled. Any effort at all applied to that right hand will have disastrous results for which I will not hold myself responsible.'

Lanny worked his neck and winced as pain shot into his shoulder. But he managed to swing his boots to the floor. He sat there; then, with a buck of his body he put his weight on his feet and jerked himself erect. He choked back a cry of pain as he swayed unsteadily for a few moments, then he sleeved sweat from his eyes and looked sourly at Doc Fogarty.

'So far so good,' he said.

Doc Fogarty shrugged. 'You lost a lot of blood. On top of that, you're trail – weary. I checked on you thoroughly, Sowarth, and I strongly advise you to lie back down and stay down for at least three days. With care – '

'I ain't lyin' down no place, Doc,' Sowarth said, no longer swaying. 'All I need now is a bottle of whiskey, and some good, solid grub. Then I'll be all right.'

Fogarty sighed wearily and turned to study the town. 'I'm no longer responsible for what happens to you, Sowarth. Please leave.'

Lanny Sowarth regarded Fogarty intently for a long time before he picked up his shirt from the end of the couch and struggled into it. The shirt had been washed clean of blood but a gaping hole showed the bandage beneath it. Sowarth put a hand over the hole, shifted his gun an inch or two about his waist and then walked to the porch steps.

'Obliged, Doc,' he said.

Doc Fogarty shook his head as Sowarth walked down the yard and into the street. It was mid – morning, and the day promised to be as hot as any that summer. He mopped his brow and wondered about Lanny Sowarth for a moment, then he went inside, put on his black hat and after locking up the cottage went into the street. He walked into Sheriff Plimpton's office minutes later and dropped wearily into a chair. Plimpton studied him curiously for a moment, wondering about Fogarty's visit. Plimpton had a lot of respect for Fogarty, though he was not the kind of man Plimpton could become friendly with. Plimpton liked a drink, a good laugh and sometimes even a down – to – earth brawl. But Fogarty struck him as the kind who would rather go into a church than a saloon.

'He's up and walking about,' Fogarty finally said.

Plimpton had come across to the desk after filling his water bag from the tank outside. He hung the bag up and watched water drip to the floor. 'Sowarth?'

Fogarty nodded. 'But he's in bad shape. I don't think you'll have to worry . . . for a couple of days at least, about him causing you any trouble.'

Plimpton grunted. 'Somebody killed his brother and he figures the man he tried to kill last night was the one who did it. He wants that man's hide more than anything in the world, so as long as he can walk and draw a gun, he'll be on the warpath. Where'd he head?'

'I didn't bother to look,' Fogarty told him.

Plimpton scowled as he picked up his gunbelt and buckled it on his huge waist. 'Why in hell didn't you look, Doc? Hell, I asked you to give me a report on him, didn't I? I'd want to know where he went when he left your place, wouldn't I? And I'd want to know what frame of mind he was in.'

Fogarty stood up, looking thoroughly bored. 'He's in bad shape, and his mind has not improved any since he came to me last night, muttering about how he was going to kill a man named Durant. As for the rest, he left my place only ten minutes ago, and he went down into the middle of the town.' Fogarty walked away from the desk and stopped in the doorway, looking out at the dusty, heat – shimmered main street. 'I'm not a deputy, Sheriff Plimpton, so please don't expect me to keep tab on men you're worried about. Find Sowarth and talk to him. For now, good day – and watch that blood pressure of yours.'

Fogarty went out to the boardwalk and Plimpton rubbed a hand over his face and swore under his breath. His blood pressure had never been better. Sure he was hot, but it was a damned hot day and anybody who wasn't sweating, as Fogarty wasn't, just wasn't normal. Plimpton crossed the jailhouse floor, closed the street door after him and strode along the boardwalk in the direction of the saloon. On his way he sighted Crane and Hap Wheeler coming from the eatery near the rooming house. He was tempted to approach them and find out what Durant was up to but stopped himself, certain he would get nothing out of that tight – lipped pair. So he turned into the saloon, still wiping sweat from his face and neck, and crossed to the bar counter. He put money down and waited impatiently for the barkeep to bring him a drink. Meantime he turned, checking out the customers.

When he saw Lanny Sowarth, sitting on his own at a card table with a bottle of whiskey in front of him, Plimpton straightened, frowning, and when his drink came, he plucked it up and pounded down the room to stop at Sowarth's table.

Lanny Sowarth looked up sullenly at him and asked, 'What the hell do you want, lawman?'

Plimpton pulled out a chair and sat down. He sipped his drink, sighed with satisfaction as the whiskey burned inside him and then sat back loosening another button on his checked shirt. 'Sowarth, you're a damn fool!'

Lanny Sowarth continued to stare sullenly at him. 'I'll prove that to be wrong, lawman.'

'No. You're a damn fool, Sowarth, because you're biting off more than you can chew. I've checked Durant out with Crane and Wheeler. They told me that during that trouble with your brother, Durant showed himself to be as fast a man with a gun as either ever saw before.'

'Then they ain't seen much,' Sowarth growled.

'Wheeler is touching sixty and he's been around, Sowarth, so he should know what he's talking about.'

'He's an old fool who hardly knows a pot from a

spoon,' Sowarth growled. 'And to boot he's a liar, as is Crane. What they told you happened out there is a pack of lies, lawman, but I don't expect you to believe that. I'm busted up and Durant's walkin' tall, so you picked his side to take.'

Plimpton's face went dark with sudden anger. He leaned forward, towering over Lanny Sowarth, his huge arms pushed within inches of Sowarth's face. 'You callin' me something, mister?' he asked gruffly.

Lanny Sowarth showed no concern at Plimpton's crowding. 'I'm sayin' what I think, lawman. Always have and always will. Now you get to hell and let a man spend his idle time as he likes. I'm doing nobody any harm, sitting here drinking.'

'You're broodin', mister, and I don't like that.'

'Then go and look at somebody else, Plimpton. You've already worried the hell out of me.'

Plimpton picked up his drink, finished it off and slammed the glass down. Then he leaned forward, his huge body looming over Sowarth's face.

'Mister, either you leave town or Durant does. And so help me, if you get notions about making trouble again, I'm gonna put you under the doc's orders and give you a bunk for a week so you can rest up properly. You hear me, damn you?'

Lanny Sowarth's eyes gleamed and his mouth worked but he said nothing. He dropped his gaze to the table finally, picked up his whiskey bottle and poured himself a drink. He didn't bother to look up when Plimpton pounded away back to the bar counter, but his head jerked up when he heard Plimpton call out, 'Durant – over here!'

Blake Durant, who had come a few paces into the saloon through the batwing doors, looked at Plimpton and then, after letting his gaze sweep over Lanny Sowarth, he crossed the room and stopped beside Plimpton, who was looking down at Sowarth, a clear warning in his green eyes.

'Seems that all the drinking I do in this town, Sheriff, is at your side,' Blake said. 'Is that the pattern for all time?'

'You saw him, didn't you?' Plimpton said.

'I saw him.'

'He swears he's still gonna get you, but the doc says his shoulder's in a bad way. No matter how fast he might have been with a gun, that shoulder is going to bring him down to size.'

'He's fast,' Blake said, remembering the draw Lanny Sowarth had almost made when the old woman was being attacked by Joe Sowarth. Fast, but not fast enough.

Plimpton frowned. 'You reckon he can take you then, in a fair fight, Durant?'

Blake shook his head. 'I didn't say that.'

'Damn you, can he? I'm askin' it now and I want a plain answer.'

Blake smiled thinly at him. 'Sheriff, you're getting yourself worked up over something that might not happen. Sowarth came off second best when he tried to gun me down. He'll drink himself into a bad mood, but he won't take the matter any further.'

'You sure, Durant?'

'I know his kind. He held sway over his brother and figured he had it made with his brother behind him. When a man has had backing all his life and it suddenly goes, he isn't half as certain of himself as he used to be. He figured it was right to tackle me despite getting proof that I had nothing to do with his brother's killing. But having failed once, he won't want to fail again.'

'He might not fail next time. You ever think of that, Durant?'

Blake nodded. 'I've thought about it, and it hasn't worried me.'

Plimpton scowled. 'Maybe you've got reason, mister. Maybe you're one of them real fast guns, on the prowl through the territory, waiting your chance to collect some more notches.'

Blake's smile left his lips. 'I'm what I am, Plimpton, no more and no less. Now, if we're going

93

to enjoy a drink together, let's talk about other things.'

'Like what?'

'Why you wear a badge, for a start.'

Plimpton gaped at him and drew slightly away. 'That's something personal, Durant. A man does what he does for reasons of his own. He doesn't have to walk about telling everybody what he thinks nights, does he?'

'So now we understand each other,' Blake said.

Plimpton studied him frowningly for a moment, then smiled thinly. 'Yeah, I guess we do. But watch Sowarth. Maybe you can handle him, Durant, and maybe you can't. If I was a betting man, I'd be putting money on you, provided it was straight out, man to man, shot for shot. But maybe it won't be that way.'

'Then you'll have the opportunity to hang him, Sheriff,' Blake said as he finished his drink and put forward money for another two. At the end of the saloon Lanny Sowarth sat, staring straight up at the two big men, his face distorted as hate built up in him.

'Who exactly is Blake Durant, Jay?'

Merle Butler sat in front of the room mirror and brushed her hair, her bosom showing over the

94

cutaway of her slip. She felt completely relaxed after a hot bath. She knew her skin shone beautifully and she knew her body had completely grasped Jay Hurwood's attention. Yet Hurwood had made no direct advances towards her. He was sitting in a chair across the room from her, looking at her, but hardly seeing her.

'A hired hand,' was Hurwood's disinterested reply.

'He looks to be better than that, Jay. He walks too proudly for a man who's used to taking orders. I got the impression that he was more used to giving orders.'

Hurwood looked up quickly, his face clouded. 'What the hell do we have to worry about Durant for? What the hell are you up to, Merle? If you figure this is gonna be another business like Sonora, think again. There isn't going to be any mixing with my hands.'

'You said they were no longer your hired help, Jay,' Merle said as she put down the brush and turned towards him, the sunlight through the window striking her in a way that softened the curves of her body.

Hurwood gasped in a quick breath, then he snapped, 'I said to forget it, Merle. I did what I said I'd do, and we got paid off, didn't we?'

Merle smiled. 'Yes, Jay, you told me to stay behind while you brought the cattle up this way. I did just that. I waited months, hardly ever going into the street because I had so little money. I couldn't even afford to enter a store. But that's finished now, Jay, isn't it? We have money, don't we?'

Hurwood patted the pocket of his shirt and grinned, 'We sure have, more than I figured to get.'

'So as soon as I dress, let's go shopping. There are so many things I've craved for.'

'Can't you wait until we take the next train out? Things are cheaper and in better supply in Cheyenne.'

Merle rose and stood before him, shaking her head. 'I can't wait any longer, Jay. I've waited too long now. The last few days I've walked the town looking at things I want and need. I'm going to have them.'

Jay Hurwood rose to his feet too and put his hands on her shoulders. But Merle drew back, again shaking her head. 'No soft talk this time, Jay. I don't trust you when you look that way and touch me that way. I want to go shopping and later, when that's done, well, you know I'm yours all the way.'

Hurwood dropped his hands and turned away. He stopped at the window and looked down into the dusty street. He was thoughtfully silent for a long time before he turned back to her and looking completely at ease, said quietly, 'All right, Merle. Get dressed. I'll call back for you in half an hour.'

'Where are you going?' she asked. 'Can't you wait for me and we'll go down together? Are you ashamed to be seen with me?'

'You know better than that, Merle. I've got a few small things to take care of and then we'll do what you want. Fifteen minutes then?'

Merle licked her lips thoughtfully and nodded. 'No longer,' she said and she crossed the room, opened a cupboard and eyed off the line of dresses hanging inside. Her face clouded as she looked at them, dresses she had worn so often she shuddered at the thought of putting one on again. She had not made her selection when she heard the door close.

Heeling about, Merle frowned at the door, uncertainty over Jay Hurwood again working through her. Since arriving in Gabriel, she thought he'd been acting strangely. For one thing, he'd released a crew he'd described as the best bunch of men he'd ever hired. Another thing, he hadn't made any advances towards her, and she couldn't believe this was because she had mentioned being mauled in Sonora after his departure. She had made it very definite that she had not been a willing partner to the business and she thought he'd believed her.

Putting on a dress, she combed her hair again and touched up her face with rouge before picking up a small handbag and leaving the room. She didn't bother to lock the door because she knew Jay Hurwood wouldn't have left any of his money there for fear that she might find it. His distrust of her she didn't mind. She felt he had good reason for feeling that way, and if she had her way, she would prove his suspicions to be perfectly correct. Smiling at this thought, she went down to the street and stopped outside the rooming house front door to survey the busy scene before her. She found Gabriel to be a quaint little town whose people appeared ordinary. She knew she'd made a big impression on many of the men folk, and she was well aware that most of the women were envious and suspicious of her.

So what? she told herself. Jay had money now, and if he wasn't the perfect man for her in many ways, the money would help her forget his failings. Later, with good clothes and jewelry, she would attract a better class of man. She might even meet the right man, somebody who looked like Blake Durant, who carried himself with self – assurance and was far more important than a mere cowhand.

Walking down the boardwalk she thought again of Durant. Her eyes brightened at the thought of having him interested in her. She could make her charms work with most men. But him? She wasn't sure. Durant seemed to be a man drawn completely within himself, a man who seemed to need no one else.

She had just passed the eatery, looking about for Jay Hurwood whom she had never intended to wait for back in her room, when she saw Durant come out of the saloon. Sheriff Plimpton was with him, looking like a huge barrel of lard to Merle. Merle touched her hair, smoothed down her dress and walked on, heading straight for them, pleased to see Plimpton turn and go up the boardwalk the other way. Merle was determined to get more than a grunt from Blake Durant this time, despite the crowded street and the time of day.

Walking briskly, she got to within ten yards of him before Blake saw her. Merle ignored the deep frown which etched into Durant's handsome face. Her mouth widened into a smile of open invitation and her eyes brightened.

'Why, Mr Durant! How nice to meet you again.'

Durant stopped in his tracks. The drinks with Plimpton had relaxed him. He'd meant to check on Sundown and perhaps make arrangements to go for a ride on him later in the day, when it cooled down. But he wanted no part of this woman whom Jay Hurwood had put his brand on.

'Miss Butler,' Blake said, touching his hat and looking past her down the boardwalk, as if something there needed his immediate attention.

But Merle put a hand on his forearm and asked, 'Have you seen Jay, Mr Durant?'

He shook his head.

'Well, he came into the street only a short time ago but I can't find him. Perhaps he's in the saloon. Would you look for me?'

'He's not in there,' Durant told her.

Merle frowned.

'I just came from there,' he said. 'Perhaps he's up the other end of the town.'

'Yes, perhaps. Will you escort me then, Mr Durant. I'm – I'm worried about the stares. You'd think I was a freak the way the men keep at it.'

Blake was aware that men who passed were looking her way. He nodded coolly and moved beside her. As he did, Lanny Sowarth stepped into the mouth of the saloon laneway. He had a gun in his hand and his face was a mask of drink – blotched hatred.

Before Blake could move to protect Merle, she gave out a sharp cry of fear. Backing away from him, she called out, 'No! No!' Then she turned and broke into a run. Blake stood his ground, his feet planted wide, while Lanny Sowarth lifted his gun.

Blake could see that he was having trouble taking perfect aim, with his shoulder dipped awkwardly and his hand shaking a great deal.

Blake said calmly, 'You'll hang for it, Sowarth. It isn't worth it.'

'Damn you, Durant! You've tricked them all, but you haven't tricked me! Who else went after my brother out there? Who else hated his guts and was scared of him?'

'The drink's got you,' Blake stalled.

'I'm clear in the head, Durant. Never been clearer. I'm gonna kill you. And I'll kill anybody who comes after me.'

Blake watched Sowarth snag the hammer of the gun back. He weighed his chances, knowing they were slim. But he didn't intend to stand there and get killed cold. He looked past Lanny Sowarth where a small crowd had gathered and it was clear from their faces that no one was going to buy into this business.

He flexed the fingers of his right hand. If Sowarth missed, he would easily cut him down. But whether he wanted to kill him or not, he didn't know. Then a shot rang out from across the street. Blake wheeled about, his gun coming into his hand in a flash. Then he saw Lanny Sowarth reeling into the laneway mouth to hit the wall with his wounded shoulder. Blood streamed down his face from a head wound, his legs buckled under him.

Another shot ripped into the laneway mouth and slammed into the wall only a few inches from Lanny Sowarth's falling body. Blake broke into a run towards Sowarth as a third and then a fourth shot sounded. He reached the laneway opening, fired a couple of loose shots across the street, and then ducked, picked up Lanny Sowarth and drew him back into the shadows. The shooting stopped then.

Lanny Sowarth stared stupidly at Durant and groaned, 'It wasn't you, Durant. It wasn't you who got me. Somebody else. Somebody else across the street. I'd – I'd just seen her and then the shot hit me.'

Blake eased him back against the wall and a shudder went through Lanny's body. His eyes closed and then his head went down on his chest. Blake held him there, conscious of a crowd gathering behind him. He looked back, but there was no sign of Merle Butler in the crowd. Then Rod Plimpton came thrusting forward, his face heavy with anger.

# SIX

# HUNTED!

'Durant!'

Plimpton stormed up to Blake who supported the unconscious Lanny Sowarth. His face scarlet, the big lawman pulled his gun and leveled it on Blake. He stood there, his huge chest rising and falling.

'By hell, you two have gone too far this time, Durant. I warned you and you didn't give a spit for what I said. Now by hell, you'll pay for this.'

'He's in a bad way,' Blake said as he stripped his bandanna from his neck and padded it against Sowarth's scalp wound.

'I don't care how he is or how you are, Durant. Get back from him right away. Give me your gun.'

Blake settled Lanny Sowarth against the wall so that he wouldn't topple over, then he came slowly to his feet. The crowd behind them had grown considerably and among the faces he recognized Crane's and Hap Wheeler's. But when they looked his way, he shook his head and although his two trail companions forced their way to the edge of the crowd, they didn't come any further.

Blake pulled out his gun and handed it to Plimpton who lifted it to his nose and sniffed.

Blake said, 'I fired two shots across the street but didn't hit anybody.'

Plimpton snorted his disbelief, pushed the gun under his belt and shoved Blake roughly against the wall. He then knelt at Lanny Sowarth's side and studied his head wound. His face tightened again when he looked back up at Durant.

'Seems you ain't the great shot you figure you are, Durant. Another half -inch and you'd have missed him altogether.'

'I didn't shoot him,' Blake said.

Plimpton's mouth tightened and his fist went white under the pressure of his grip on his gun. He jerked up to his feet and snarled, 'Damn you, I've had enough lies!'

'Somebody must have seen it,' Durant said calmly. 'It happened out there on the boardwalk.

Sowarth was coming for me, sure, but before he could get a bead on me, somebody from across the street started shooting. The first shot hit Sowarth in the head and he went down. The other shots threatened to tear him apart, so I pulled him into cover.'

Plimpton's mouth gaped and his stare narrowed. 'Enough of it, damn you, Durant! What the hell do you take me for?'

'It's like he just said, Sheriff,' a voice came down to them. Turning, Rod Plimpton stared into the grizzled face of an old – timer. He was backed by four other men, one a tall, businesslike young man who put in:

'Rod, that's how it was. Durant was coming down the street with that new woman when suddenly she screamed. I guess that was what made us look Durant's way. Then some shots came from across the street and that feller was hit and knocked back into this laneway. There were other shots then, and finally Durant opened fire – mostly, I reckon to give himself some cover. He then disappeared in here and I guess he did what he just said, and dragged that feller into cover.'

Plimpton swore savagely under his breath and spun on Durant again. 'Who was across the street then?'

'I didn't see him.'

'What do you mean you didn't see him? Do you shoot at flies, mister?'

Blake stood against the wall and held Plimpton's stare locked in his own. 'The sun was in my eyes. Anyway, whoever it was, he was in the laneway mouth near the bank and that big store. I had no chance of seeing him, let alone hitting him.'

Plimpton glared at the old – timer and his younger companion and then snapped, 'You tellin' the truth? You ain't just backin' Durant because he stands so damn almighty proud and sure of himself?'

The old – timer shook his head. 'Plimpton, we've got no cause to lie and you've got no cause to doubt us or shoot your mouth off. By hell, lately I reckon that badge is gettin' to you. Time you learned that—'

'Go to hell!' Plimpton said angrily and to back his words he waved his gun about wildly, stepping towards the ring of men and brandishing the gun in their faces. 'All of you – get! Every damn one of you.'

Dave Crane and Hap Wheeler moved out of Plimpton's way but went no further than the edge of the saloon wall. They stood there then looking directly at Blake Durant as if waiting for some word from him. But Durant had knelt at Lanny Sowarth's side again and was wiping blood from his face. Lanny Sowarth was still unconscious and his face was chalky white.

'He won't make it if left here,' Blake said. He worked his hands under the limp body and then lifted Sowarth in his arms. Plimpton, now that the crowd had drawn back, wheeled around to glare furiously at Blake. But then he calmed.

'OK. Get him to Fogarty's. Then, Durant, you stay there. I want to talk some more to you and by hell you'd better have some real sweet answers.'

Blake ignored the outburst as he walked with the limp Lanny Sowarth in his arms. But, as he stepped into the sunlight of the street, his stare swung across to the mouth of the bank laneway. The lane was deserted, as he'd expected it to be. His stare then moved down the street in the direction of the rooming house. But there was no sign of Merle Butler. Seeing Crane and Hap Wheeler trailing him, Blake crossed the street and went up the boardwalk to Doc Fogarty's office. He found the doctor waiting on his porch. Pulling Sowarth's head up, he inspected the head wound and gave a grunt. 'Wouldn't be told,' he muttered. 'Damn loco.'

He then walked through the porch doorway into the house, leaving Blake to follow. In the sick – room, Fogarty carelessly pointed to a bunk against the wall and filled a basin with steaming water. He then eased Blake aside, saying, 'Wait outside.'

Blake left the room, returned to the porch and stood leaning against the overhang, one hand stretched high above his head. When Hap Wheeler and Dave Crane reached the steps leading to the porch, Blake's look went to them, but the thoughtful look in his eyes kept them from asking him questions. So the three of them stood there, watching Rod Plimpton come from the mouth of the bank laneway, the gun still in his big hand, his shoulders stooped, and his worried look sweeping the street.

Merle Butler didn't stop running until she reached her room, where she slammed the door shut, threw home the bolt and then leaned against the wall, strands of hair plastered to her cheeks, her hands shaking and fear still fixed in her eyes. She stood there, trembling all over and scarcely able to get her breath.

'No,' she murmured. 'It – it just couldn't be!'

But there was nobody in the room to agree or argue with her. After a time, she crossed to the mirror and began combing her hair. But her hands were still trembling so much she couldn't do it properly so she threw the comb down in disgust and crossed to the window. From there she could see down into the street where all seemed normal again.

There was a knock on the door and Merle swung about, her mouth open, her eyes big. A second knock came, followed by, 'Are you all right, Miss Butler? It's Cameron.'

Cameron? Merle didn't have any idea who Cameron was. He might be a friend of the man in the street for all she knew.

'I'm the clerk, Miss Butler. I talked to you some last night – said if there was anything you wanted, just to ask for it. You want something now?'

The foyer clerk! Merle breathed a sigh of relief. The fool of a man had been impudent enough to suggest they might have a drink together in a back room. She hadn't openly refused him, because she never closed all doors on herself. But the look of him and the smell of him was enough to make her positive that he would be the very last straw.

Merle opened the door and stepped back to let Cameron come in. He looked deeply concerned as he looked intently at her. 'I saw you come in, Miss Butler. You were sure in a hurry. Something bother you in the street?'

'It was just . . . just something personal. You don't have to worry about it. But I would like a drink if you could find one.'

'Sure, sure,' Cameron said, his face lighting up. 'Got a bottle under the counter. I'll go get it.'

A moment later Merle heard him running down the stairs. She was more composed now, and after a drink she knew she would be able to think clearly again. How had that man got to Gabriel? Did he come along with Jay Hurwood from Sonora? But that night in Sonora he had told her that he was staying behind, that he was sick of riding the trails and wanted some town comforts. She hadn't believed him to be the kind who would settle in a town, but he had been well – mannered and he'd said he had a lot of money. It was only when the other one arrived, the one who had . . .

Merle shuddered again and put her face in her trembling hands. The very thought of that night unnerved her completely. She had never been so roughly handled, and with Jay off with his cattle she'd had nobody to turn to.

Cameron came back, slipped silently into the room and closed the door behind him. Crossing to the washbasin, he began to pour whiskey into two glasses. When he smiled at Merle, she thought she'd be sick. Then Cameron handed her a drink, saying, 'We'd best not make too much noise. I'm not supposed to be up with the guests, not womenfolk anyway. Just a drink or two and we'll talk some and you can tell me what your trouble is. You'll find Bose Cameron is just the man to fix it for you, no matter what it is.'

Merle took the drink and turned back to the window again. She swirled the whiskey in the glass and then lifted the glass and drained it in a gulp. Cameron gaped as he sipped his own whiskey and felt it burning down to his stomach. Merle handed the glass back and he filled it again. This time Merle merely held the glass at her bosom and stared thoughtfully down the street.

'Where's your friend?' Cameron asked.

Merle looked across her shoulder at him. 'What friend?'

'The one who came up here last night – feller brought in a bunch of cattle last night.'

Merle shrugged. 'How should I know?'

Cameron grinned and moved closer to her. He changed his glass to his left hand and slipped his right arm about her waist. Merle went rigid and wheeled away from him. Cameron looked shocked and opened his mouth to speak – just as the door was flung open and Jay Hurwood came storming into the room.

Cameron almost dropped his glass in shock. He stood there shaking his head as Jay Hurwood, after a savage look at Merle, went straight for Cameron and without a word grabbed him by the shoulder and pulled him towards the doorway. Cameron began to protest his innocence but Jay Hurwood hurled him through the doorway and then kicked the door closed.

'Don't come back!' he shouted.

Merle watched him blankly as he threw home the bolt and turned on her. She said, 'You're a damn fool, Jay. I was feeling poorly and that man offered me a drink. Naturally I accepted it.'

'You can't help yourself,' Hurwood growled sourly as he crossed the room. He studied the bottle for a moment and then lifted it and drank. He coughed when he swallowed too much, then he put the bottle down and wiped his mouth on his sleeve. He went to the window, easing Merle roughly aside, and then he looked down at the street.

'Did you see what happened out there?' Merle asked.

'I saw it.'

'I was looking for you, Jay, and one of those scum, one of the two I told you about from Sonora, stepped in front of me. I recognized him right off and almost collapsed with fright.'

Jay Hurwood studied her bitterly, his mouth twisted. 'You looked anything but on the verge of collapsing, holding onto Durant's arm, damn you!'

Some color rose into Merle's fair – skinned face. 'Mr Durant was helping me look for you, Jay. For God's sake, can't you believe anything?'

'I can't believe you or trust you, Merle. Damned if I know why I put up with you.'

Merle's face tightened with anger. 'You put up with me because I'm all you ever wanted. You married my sister, Jay, and she wasn't good enough for you when you saw me. You had to have me, and you did everything you could to get me. You didn't care about your friendships, your business associates, or your wife. You cared about nothing but me and that's how it will always be.'

Hurwood walked across to her and looked angrily into her eyes. Then he nodded grimly, 'Yeah, you've got a curse on me all right, Merle. Damn you for that!'

His hand cracked across her face, knocking her down to the bed. Merle let out a sharp cry and covered her face with her hands. Jay Hurwood took another drink. When Merle finally dropped her hands and looked fearfully at him, she saw that he was smiling. She swore at him.

'Don't go sniffing about Durant's heels, or the clerk's heels or anybody else's heels,' he said. 'And while we're in town, you stay in this room. I'll get you anything you like. As for shopping here, forget it. You can do your shopping in Cheyenne when we get there, which won't be too long.'

Merle sat up, her face flushed. Hurwood had often struck her but he'd never really hurt her. Apart from a few slaps, she could twist him around her fingers, and if she handled it carefully enough she could always get what she wanted from him. The sting of his blow had already gone when she said, 'I just said I saw one of those men I told you about, Jay. I thought you'd fired them.'

Jay Hurwood looked keenly at her. 'How could I fire them when I didn't know who they were.'

'But the other evening, after you'd seen Mr Thomas and made arrangements to sell your cattle, I mentioned it to you. I described them and I told you I was positive they were two you'd hired in Sonora to make the trip with you.'

'That was the night before I returned to my outfit, Merle, only two days ago.'

Merle looked puzzled. She got to her feet and approached him. There was no fear in her face now, only a deep – seated worry.

'Jay, if you knew who they were then, and knew what they'd done to me, why didn't you react in some way?'

Jay Hurwood smiled thinly. 'I did react.'

His tone brought new concern into Merle's dark eyes. 'How?'

'I killed one of them, and just awhile ago I shot the other one.'

Merle reeled away from him, horrified, shaking her head so hard that her hair flew about her face. 'No, Jay!' she said. 'Not – not killing!'

'They mauled you, you said. They were supposed to be with the cattle but they came into town. I must have missed them on my way out. Next morning they told me they'd gone back to town for a last drinking bout and I believed them. So I kept them on and knew nothing of what had happened to you until the other night. Then, with my cattle already close enough to town for me to bring them in on my own if necessary, and with a storm blowing like all hell out there, I ran into one of them and put it to him. He went for his gun and I shot him.'

Merle sank back on the bed, her eyes closed and her body quivering. 'No,' she said.

'The other one I meant to settle with here in town, but things happened and it looked like he'd be taken care of by Durant. Only that blasted Durant got some holy stuff into his head and wouldn't finish him off. Now you've run into him and he knows you're in town. It won't take long for him to work out what's been happening and who killed his brother. There are going to be some storms brewing, Merle, which is why you're going to stay in this room and keep the door locked at all times. Do you hear me?'

Merle looked anxiously up at him, and Hurwood frowned heavily, never having seen her so distraught before. He crossed to her and took her trembling hands.

'They deserved to die,' he said. 'I couldn't let them live, not when I knew what they'd done to you.'

Merle withdrew her hands with a jerk and drew away from him. 'Not killing, Jay. I've never been caught up in a thing like that.'

Hurwood became angry again. 'You've been caught up in a lot of things, damn you, so a little bloodshed shouldn't worry you. Don't worry – I'll handle everything from here. But remember – you stay in this room until I'm ready to pull out. We'll forget the train. I'll buy a rig and get us a good horse. We can have a pleasant trip back to Cheyenne.'

Merle looked away from him but not before he saw deep anguish in her face. He couldn't understand that, and he wasn't sure if he could trust her. So he said, in a voice filled with tenderness, 'Merle, we'll make it. I said I'd make money and I did. I risked everything I had for you and I'll go on risking it until I have enough money to set you up comfortably for life. So what have you got to worry about?'

Merle brought her troubled gaze back to him and shook her head. 'I don't know, Jay. I'm all confused and upset. I need another drink.'

Hurwood picked the bottle up off the table and took it across to her. Handing it to her, he said, 'Drink all you like – only stay here, Merle. I'm going down into the town now to see what's happening about the shooting. Nobody saw me shoot down Sowarth, so there won't be any danger. I'll just act as I'll be expected to act. I'll tie up some loose business ends, get that rig and horse and pack it with what we'll need for the trip. A day or two from now, we'll be in open country with not a worry in the world.'

Merle took the bottle and poured herself a drink. Then she sat forward, staring at the whiskey in the glass. She had never been a good drinker, but she felt right then that she could empty the bottle and drink another and not feel its effects. Hurwood went to the door, opened it, and turned back.

'You all right now, Merle?'

Merle nodded without looking at him.

'OK. I won't be long.

Jay Hurwood closed the door behind him and checked out the passageway. Finding it empty, he went down the foyer stairway and approached the desk. Bose Cameron looked nervously at him, but Hurwood merely said, 'Keep away from her, mister, and see that nobody bothers her. She's had a hard time of it lately.'

Cameron nodded grimly. 'I was only trying to help.'

'Sure. But from now on, be smart,' Hurwood said, then he left the rooming house and walked along the boardwalk. Having used the back street and the backyard of the rooming – house, he was confident he hadn't been seen shooting Lanny Sowarth. He entered the saloon and ordered a drink, looking easily about him, but he knew no one but the cattle buyer, Roger Thomas. Hurwood crossed the room to the buyer, and then, smiling, asked if he could join him. Thomas introduced him to the train guards to whom he was giving last instructions about the care of the cattle on the journey to the eastern market. Hurwood sipped his drink, loosened his string tie and relaxed.

Doc Fogarty came onto the porch wiping his hands with a towel. He looked at Hap Wheeler and Dave Crane and walked to where Blake Durant was leaning against the porch rail.

'He'll be all right,' Fogarty said. 'That business opened his shoulder wound again and he lost a lot more blood. But the head wound is only shallow and will cause no more inconvenience than some bad headaches for awhile. After that he should be all right.'

Blake thanked him and asked, 'How long will he be laid up here with you?'

Fogarty shook his head. 'I'd like to keep him for a couple of days, and I will if he has no objections. But he's already proved that he's not willing to take my advice. He'll be unconscious and too weak to move for the rest of today, but by morning I expect he'll be up and about and straining to get going.'

Blake walked to the top of the porch steps where Wheeler and Crane were still waiting for him. He was about to go down when Rod Plimpton came along the boardwalk and signaled for the three of them to stay put. He came into the cottage yard then and walked stiffly up to the steps. After getting information on Sowarth's condition from Fogarty, Plimpton turned to Durant.

'I've made a further check on what happened and it seems you saved Sowarth's life. Now why in hell would you do that?'

'He's no threat to me,' Blake said.

119

Plimpton's eyes popped wide with feigned surprise. 'No? He jumps up in front of you, gun in hand and ready to shoot your guts out – and you reckon he's no threat to you?'

'He knows better now,' Blake told him.

'Like what?'

'Like somebody else wants him dead, not me.'

Plimpton studied Blake intently. 'Put that clearer, mister.'

Blake rested a hand on the overhang post. 'Sheriff, Lanny Sowarth believed all along that I'd killed his brother. Now he knows I saved his life. Why would I do that except to prove my innocence? Even with the way his mind works, he can't deny my innocence now. He won't worry me again.'

Plimpton asked, 'Do you know who killed his brother?'

Blake shook his head. 'No.'

Plimpton scowled at him and turned to Wheeler and Crane. 'Maybe you pair do. Maybe somebody here has begun to put two and two together, eh?'

Hap Wheeler shook his head, but Dave Crane, looking intently at Blake Durant, gave no answer of any kind. Plimpton noticed this and kept at him.

'You, cowboy, have you got any ideas?'

Crane dragged his troubled gaze back to Plimpton. 'No, Sheriff, I don't know anything. I'm ready to hit the trail and get to blazes away from this town and away from Sowarth. Unlike Durant, I don't think he's right in the head.'

Plimpton cursed under his breath, then turned and walked down the pathway to the street. Outside the gate he stopped again, and when Blake drew up he said, 'I've got it figured this way, Durant. Whoever killed Sowarth's brother figured you'd take care of Sowarth. But he didn't figure on your damned stubbornness and your contrary ways. The killer, once he found out you weren't out to shoot Sowarth, took things into his own hands and tried to finish Sowarth off. What I want to know is – why? When I know that, I'll know who.'

Blake looked back at him. 'I only knew the Sowarth boys for three weeks, and we were on the trail all that time. So I have no way of knowing if they'd done something to cause a man to track them down. An avenger.'

'An avenger, eh?'

'Somebody out to even a score, Sheriff. If you knew those two as I got to know them, you'd find it easy to believe they'd left plenty of enemies behind them. But outside of that, I don't know a damned thing.'

Plimpton sighed wearily and then he looked at Hap Wheeler and Dave Crane. He got nothing from their faces and went on his way without another word. But halfway across the street, he stopped to glance back and seemed about to return to them. Instead, however, he wheeled about and went on his way.

Dave Crane said, 'What the hell's going on, Durant? You got any idea?'

'Some,' Blake told him and looked thoughtfully up the street towards the rooming house.

'Then maybe you'll let us in on it, eh?' Crane suggested.

Blake shrugged. 'I don't know enough, in fact I don't have anything but suspicions to work on. Let's have a drink on it.'

'Best thing said today,' put in Hap Wheeler and the three of them crossed the sunlit street and went into the saloon.

# SEVEN

# PULLING OUT

Jay Hurwood rose from Thomas' table when he saw Durant, Crane and Wheeler enter the saloon. He mumbled his apologies to Thomas and his companions and made his way to the bar counter. Durant pushed forward money for drinks and leaned on the counter's edge staring into the bar mirror, seeing Hurwood coming towards him. The drinks came and Durant turned slowly to give Hurwood a casual look.

Hurwood nodded at Durant. 'I just heard about Sowarth. He's still at it, is he?'

'Seems like,' Blake said.

'Blasted damn fool! Can't he be made to understand? I know it's none of my business, Durant, but you worked well for me. You gave me no trouble and perhaps I was a bit hasty in washing my hands of all this trouble. You want me to go see Sowarth and talk to him?'

'What could you say to him?' Blake asked.

Hurwood shrugged his heavy shoulders and pursed his lips thoughtfully. 'Well, maybe he'd listen to me. I was, after all, the man who hired him. I gave him his brother's pay dirt, too, so maybe he'll feel obligated to me. I'd like to ride out knowing everything was peaceful behind me.'

'It might work,' Dave Crane put in. 'Then we could hit a fresh trail, Durant.'

Blake nodded. 'I can't see how it could do any harm, Hurwood. But you'll have to wait awhile. He's still unconscious and the doctor says he won't be feeling like talking to anybody until tomorrow morning at the earliest.. Thanks.'

Hurwood nodded grimly and finished his drink. Then he reached out and put some money on the counter. 'Get the drinks, Crane, while I talk to Durant privately, will you?'

Crane nodded his willingness to do this and Hurwood, taking Blake's arm, drew away from the other two. He went several yards along the bar and then breathed in deeply.

'Durant, you've seen the woman who is with me,

haven't you?'

Blake nodded.

'She means a great deal to me.'

'So?'

'So, when I heard that Sowarth was hurt while she was walking the street with you, I didn't like it.'

'What part of it Hurwood?'

Hurwood frowned. 'The part about you and her being together, Durant. Merle is a fine woman in lots of ways, but she's too easily attracted to men like you. She means no harm, I know, but men get the wrong idea about her friendliness. I wouldn't want you to get the wrong idea, Durant.'

Blake smiled thinly at him. 'You needn't worry on that score, Hurwood. I don't know her and I don't wish to.'

'Easily said,' Hurwood murmured.

'And easily believed, Hurwood,' Blake told him with a hint of annoyance coming into his voice.

Hurwood accepted this with a terse nod. 'Well, for the moment I'll believe that. We'll be moving out anyway, when the air cools down. Just do me a favor, will you, and keep away from her. It appears I've said too much about you to her already and she's curious to know more, if you get what I mean.'

'No, I don't,' Blake said and eased Hurwood aside. He made his way back to Wheeler and Crane and accepted the drink Crane offered him. Crane had another glass extended in Hurwood's direction, but Hurwood had turned and gone the other way.

'The less the merrier,' Hap said. 'So enjoy Jay Hurwood's hospitality finally. I never thought he'd get around to it.'

Blake Durant stood there, looking thoughtfully after the big cattle dealer while Crane and Wheeler counted out the money Hurwood had left for them.

'Seven dollars,' Crane announced.

Blake Durant finished his drink and studied each of them in turn. Then he said, 'Whoever tried to kill Lanny Sowarth may have another try.'

Hap Wheeler grunted at this and Crane straightened.

'So what, Durant?'

'So we rode with Sowarth and his brother.'

'Which doesn't make us kin,' Wheeler put in.

'No, Hap, it doesn't. But can you ride on, not knowing?'

'Not knowing what?'

'Who killed Joe Sowarth and why. And who wants Lanny Sowarth under the ground too.'

Wheeler cursed under his breath. 'It don't matter an owlhoot to me. Neither of them two ever said a kind word to me, or ever acted like anything better

126

than rattlers.'

'A third attempt could be made on Lanny Sowarth's life today,' Blake said.

Wheeler straightened, his old face creased with annoyance. 'So we buy into the business, Durant? Is that what you've got in mind?'

Blake shrugged. 'I'm just saying it's hard for any man to ride on and leave a mystery behind him. For mine, I've got a little something to work on. While I'm doing that, I'd like to be assured that Lanny's life isn't in danger. Maybe he deserves most of the pain that's come his way, but what man deserves to be killed cold?'

Dave Crane put down his drink and wiped his mouth. 'You want somebody at doc's, watching over Sowarth, Durant?'

Blake nodded. 'It might reveal to us who's after Sowarth's hide. That known, life would be a lot simpler for all of us.'

Dave Crane nodded. 'Hell, my head's been bustin' with thinkin' about it all the damned time. I reckon I can't ride away, not knowing. What about you, Hap?'

Hap Wheeler grunted under his breath, finished off his drink and studied Blake Durant. 'What do you know, Durant, that we don't?'

Blake shook his head. 'Nothing much, Hap.'

'Well, if you're gonna be so tight – fisted, you'd best handle it all by yourself, big man.'

Blake smiled at him. 'I'll let you think about it, Hap. I don't think anything will happen until evening anyway. It would be too risky for a killer to show himself in daylight. Drink well, Hap – I've had enough.'

With that, Blake Durant left. He returned to his room and locked the door; and then, as he had done so often in the past, he lay there looking at the ceiling and thinking about the one woman he had loved, Louise Yerby.


Lanny Sowarth blinked his eyes. Evening had brought coolness into his room. He'd tried to move a few times but the effort brought excruciating pain. So he lay completely still, the pain in his head so bad that he had forgotten about his shoulder wound.

The door opened and Doc Fogarty came into the room. He carried a lantern which he put on the table beside Sowarth's bunk. Without a word he went out again, but he returned a few minutes later with a bowl of steaming broth that he set on the table.

'Can you sit up?' Fogarty asked.

Lanny Sowarth scowled and said nothing.

'You've got to eat, Sowarth, or you'll waste away and die. But I'll leave that up to you.'

Doc went out to the porch in time to see Sheriff Rod Plimpton coming up the pathway. It was Plimpton's third visit that day.

Drawing to a halt at the bottom of the yard steps Plimpton took off his hat and mopped his brow. He looked deeply worried. 'How is he, Doc?'

'Eating.'

Plimpton showed surprise. 'He's a tough little runt, eh?'

'He's determined to get well and on his feet. I don't understand men like him, wanting to fight all the time. What makes them tick?'

Rod Plimpton shook his head. 'Some are born loco. Or maybe they had it bad when growing up and so they carry a burn against the whole world. This one, though, he's got something else burning him up.'

'Revenge?' Fogarty asked.

'Yeah, revenge, Doc. How long do you reckon it'll be before he can move about?'

'I'd say by morning, the way he's pushing himself. He won't be much of a threat to anybody, though.'

'Well, if he skips out on you, let me know right away, will you? There's more in this damned thing than Sowarth going after Durant. I don't know what, but I'm damned if I can sleep until I find out. You'll do that for me, Doc?'

Fogarty nodded. Plimpton went on his way and Dave Crane and Hap Wheeler appeared at the side of the house. Fogarty signaled them to come onto the porch. After waiting until Plimpton was out of sight down the dark street, they climbed the steps.

Fogarty said, 'He won't be back tonight. Where do you want to wait?'

'Out here, Doc,' Wheeler said. 'That way we won't be under your feet.'

'As you wish, Mr Wheeler,' Fogarty said. 'But remember your promise to me. You won't do any killing unless it's impossible to avoid.'

'I ain't about to forget, Doc. You handled Plimpton good.'

Fogarty grunted, then went back inside. He checked on Lanny Sowarth and found him lying on his back again. The bowl was empty. Fogarty picked it up and went out, closing the bedroom door after him. He felt tired after so much activity during the day. But it was a weariness he welcomed and succumbed to, for he had two guards outside.

He kicked off his boots and stretched out on his bunk and was soon fast asleep.

*

'We'll go down by way of Temple Creek, Merle. That way I'll be able to look in on some old friends who might be able to tell me the state of the market in Lusc and Fresno Creek. I don't see any sense in making all this money and then spending it. I want to turn it over a couple of times, maybe three times, then head for the Capitol.'

Hurwood rose, putting a map into his shirt pocket. He crossed to where Merle was lying on her back, her face flushed with drink. Her eyes were closed and her regular breathing told him that she was in a deep sleep. He sat beside her on the bed and picked up her left hand. Looking at it he marveled at the smoothness of it. Her sister had had rough hands due to all the hard work she had done in her life. But somehow Merle had managed to avoid work. Hurwood wasn't stupid enough to deny the fact that Pat, Merle's sister was the better woman. But she didn't have the zest for living and the need for excitement that made Merle so alluring to him. Pat was a good woman who deserved a good man. It was unfortunate that he wasn't that man.

Standing, he went to the window and looked down at the dark street. He had no feelings at all about Gabriel. It was just another town which had been good in a business sense to him. He had

131

changed a few brands, picked up a few strays and built his original herd of three hundred cattle up to seven hundred and fifty. He'd been lucky with his choice of hands, although the Sowarth brothers had complicated things a little. But Joe was dead, and he'd died knowing that playing about with Jay Hurwood's woman was something only a fool would do.

Now there was only Lanny, the younger brother, whom Durant hadn't shot down when he had every right to do so. Durant was an idiot in Hurwood's estimation, although he granted that Durant was no dude. He'd travelled wide and far and had learned a great deal. He was hard and tough and evidently he could use a gun well. But that didn't worry Jay Hurwood.

He went back to the bed, leaned over and kissed Merle on the cheek. She stirred and her eyes opened. She looked at him, smiled dreamily, and as he moved closer her lips parted. At that moment he was tempted to stay a while and enjoy her, but then he reminded himself that he had things to do – things which had to be done.

He said, 'I won't be long. You sleep a little more, then we'll leave town. I've got everything ready.'

Merle looked wide – eyed at him. 'What are you going to do, Jay?'

'What I have to – no more and no less.' He kissed her again. 'Sleep now,' he said, and then he went to the door. But as he opened it and stood peering down the passageway, he heard her stirring on the bed. Looking back with a slight frown, he saw her getting to her feet. She swayed a little before giving him a worried look.

'I don't like it, Jay. One is enough,' she said.

Hurwood slammed the door shut and hurried back to her.

Easing her back down on the bed, he said, 'He'll know now. He'll come for me.'

'He's nothing but a stupid little cowhand,' she argued. 'Let's go now and be rid of them.'

Hurwood looked thoughtfully at her without speaking. 'I can't.'

'You have to. For my sake you have to. I don't like killing, Jay. The other one was the worst. He mauled me, hit me, and he would have torn me apart if the other one hadn't stopped him. The worst one is dead and what happened doesn't matter anymore. You said we were packed and ready to go. So let's go.'

Hurwood pursed his lips, crossed to the window and looked down at the street again. He thought it out carefully. Nobody had a single clue that it was he who wanted Lanny Sowarth dead.

Turning, he said, 'All right. Get your things together.'

Merle's face brightened and she starred to collect her clothes. She packed them into a case. Hurwood paced impatiently while she went to the dresser and stuffed articles into the top of the case, he went across and did the job for her. He was already packed. Taking both cases, he led the way from the room, down the steps and across the foyer. Cameron came from behind the desk and studied him curiously.

Hurwood pulled out a roll of bills, paid for the room and then looked up at the clock. 'We'll get twenty miles behind us in the cool of the night,' he said.

Then he took Merle's arm and steered her out to the yard. Cameron eyed them, staring at Merle's swaying hips. He rubbed a hand over his face and swore under his breath.

'Too bad,' he said. 'Too damn bad.'

In the yard, Hurwood helped Merle into the rig, put the cases in back, then climbed up to the driving seat. Smiling, he turned the rig out of the yard and along the rooming house laneway into the front street and under the street lights. Merle leaned against him, her head on his shoulder. Hurwood put an arm about her. He could hear noise from the saloon, and he saw men watching along the boardwalk. He turned the rig out of the main street and headed along the narrow trail to Temple Creek.

Blake Durant entered the rooming house the back way and made his way up to Merle Butler's room. He had earlier discovered the number of her room from Cameron. Reaching it, he checked out the passageway before he rapped lightly. When there was no answer, he knocked louder.

Durant tried the doorknob. It turned in his hand. He opened the door, lit a match and walked in. The room was empty. Blake left the room and stood in the passageway thinking. It was clear to him that when Merle Butler had seen Lanny Sowarth in the street prior to Sowarth being cut down, she had recognized him and had been terrified of him. Why? The question had been in his mind ever since the incident. Now he wanted to know where Merle had gone.

He went down to the foyer and found Cameron standing behind his desk looking bored.

'Have you seen Miss Butler?' Blake asked.

Cameron nodded. 'Sure have.'

'Where is she?'

'Gone.'

'Gone where?'

'Left with Hurwood half an hour ago. Hurwood put her into a rig and drove out of town. He headed north.'

Blake Durant frowned and moved across to the desk. 'You couldn't have made a mistake, could you?'

'No, Durant. I've been watching that little filly about as much as you have and likely with the same thoughts. She's gone all right and my whole week's ruined.'

Blake turned and stared frowningly out at the street. It didn't fit. He had worked it out that since Merle Butler had been terrified of Lanny Sowarth, it stood to reason that she had known him before. And since she was connected with Jay Hurwood, then it was only natural that Hurwood knew the reason behind Merle's fear. It was just as reasonable to expect that Hurwood also knew Joe Sowarth from the past.

Blake Durant left the rooming house and strode along the boardwalk to Doc Fogarty's place. He wasn't sure if both Wheeler and Crane had followed his wishes and were keeping a check on Lanny Sowarth, but he felt that Crane would be on guard. He liked Crane and maybe he'd ride some trails with him.

Entering the Fogarty yard, he saw movement up on the porch. A moment later, as he walked up the pathway, a voice said, 'Far enough. Don't move now.'

Blake recognized Wheeler's gruff voice.

'It's me, Hap,' he said. 'Durant.'

He moved forward slowly, seeing another figure loom out of the deep darkness of the porch. Then Hap Wheeler and Dave Crane were standing there together, guns trained on him.

'Sowarth all right?' Durant asked.

Hap Wheeler nodded. 'Sure. He's sleeping like a baby.'

'An ugly one,' Crane put in.

Blake turned and looked down the street. 'Hurwood's left town,' he said.

Hap Wheeler drew beside him. 'Then he was the one you suspected, Durant?'

'I can't see it any other way. Nobody came into this town after the storm. And only our outfit was out on the plains. The old woman was killed and then Joe Sowarth. Then Hurwood showed up with Joe Sowarth's body.'

'But why?' Wheeler asked.

'I don't know,' Blake said. 'But I do know that Lanny Sowarth knew Hurwood's woman before he came to this town. She was terrified of him when

137

she saw him in the street. I was watching Lanny closely, too, and he recognized her and forgot momentarily about me. If the shooting hadn't started then, he would have killed her, right in front of my eyes.'

Wheeler leaned against the rail, looking suddenly very tired. 'It's still one hell of a mess,' he said.

'Sure is,' Crane agreed. But neither offered any solution to the problem.

'So we disregard Jay Hurwood,' Blake said. 'Who else is there?'

Crane and Wheeler shook their heads. Blake moved restlessly up and down the verandah for some time before he went down the porch steps into the yard. 'No sense in staying here then,' he said. 'I'm sorry I wasted your night, Hap. You, too, Dave.'

'No worry,' Crane said.

'Hold on,' Hap grunted. 'Fogarty said that Sowarth was bellyachin' about you the first time he was here, but this time he was bellyachin' about Hurwood. That make sense, Durant?'

'Some,' Blake said. 'And that's a good reason why Hurwood would want Lanny out of the way.'

'Maybe he figures he's better off running. Maybe he saw us standing guard and took fright. I don't know and I don't much care any longer. I'm finding a bunk and getting these old feet up.'

Hap Wheeler went into the darkness. Blake Durant and Dave Crane crossed the street towards the rooming house where Durant went to his own room. He felt something of a fool because he hadn't approached Merle Butler early enough and because he had ruined the night for Wheeler and Crane. In the morning he would have to work out new plans for himself. He was positive that Lanny Sowarth now knew who had killed his brother, so Blake left it at that. It was no longer his business.

# EIGHT

# THE TIGHTENING REINS

Lanny Sowarth propped himself up carefully in his bed and swung his feet to the floor. He sat there with sweat running down his face. Having just heard the conversation between Durant, Wheeler and Crane, he knew that Hurwood had left town. So he couldn't do otherwise than follow him, no matter what it took out of him.

Slowly putting his weight on his feet, he held back a groan as pain worked through his head, neck and shoulder. His throat was so dry he could hardly swallow and he felt weak in the legs. But he managed to cross the room to where Fogarty had laid out his old clothes. The hole in his shirt reminded him of Durant's bullet thudding into him, but he felt no bitterness towards Durant now. He had dogged his trail and he'd meant to kill him, only to come off second best twice in one week. But now he knew that Durant had had nothing to do with Joe's death. The guilty man was Hurwood, returning after seeing his woman and likely filled with the story of what happened back in Sonora.

Lanny cursed his brother. The woman clearly hadn't wanted either of them, despite the way she had looked their way many times, even when Hurwood had been present. Lanny had tried to get Joe to forget all about her, but Joe, once attracted by a woman, couldn't control himself.

So they had doubled back on the trail out of Sonora and had found her alone in the cottage. Joe had a bottle of whiskey with him and when Merle Butler wouldn't drink and told them to get out, Joe had pulled her head back and poured the whiskey down her throat. Merle had scratched his face and Joe had hit her, knocking her onto the divan. Then, enraged, Joe had torn her clothes off. The screams of the woman had made Lanny force Joe out of the house, but only after Joe had mauled her badly.

Then it had been back to camp and the hard,

long wait, wondering if she would ride out and tell Hurwood. She hadn't and the drive had gone on until she had turned up here in Gabriel.

Lanny put it all together as he dressed. She had told Hurwood about her trouble with them in Sonora. Hurwood had returned and killed Joe. Then, when Lanny had gone after Durant, not wanting to listen to any excuses, Hurwood had expected Durant to cut him down.

Only Durant hadn't done that. Lanny wiped heavy sweat from his face and a chill went through him. He knew he was sick, but he had a picture in his mind of Harwood bringing the dead Joe back to camp and claiming to have found his body.

Lanny opened the door, his gun at the ready. But the place was deserted. He went onto the porch and breathed in the cool night air. After several moments his head cleared, and although a throbbing pain still persisted across his brow he drew himself tall and walked silently down into the town. He made his way to the livery stable, not caring who saw him. He was leaving to hunt Hurwood down and he didn't expect to be coming back this way. The only thing that mattered was that Hurwood got his guts blasted out. Lanny Sowarth was ready to die when he saw that happen.

He worked his way about the horse yard at the

livery stable until he found his horse. It was a high – backed roan with plenty of speed in its tail and lots of stamina after the two – day layoff. He led it back into the stable where the attendant, hearing the noise, came out with his shotgun.

Lanny brushed him aside, saying, 'It's my horse and you were paid a week in advance.'

With that he threw his saddle on the roan, fastened it in place and then struggled into the saddle. The attendant, although he had lowered his gun, remained in the doorway watching him.

'You're Sowarth, aren't you, the one everybody's been shooting at?'

Lanny looked down at him. 'You want to join the mob, mister?'

The attendant quickly drew back, shaking his head. 'Hell, no. But, mister, you look bad. You look real bad. If you don't have to ride out, I reckon I've got space out back for you and some coffee on the boil. Whyn't you rest up? No man has to ride lookin' and feelin' like you do.'

Lanny swung the roan's head past the man's shoulder and let the horse walk. He turned out of the yard and headed for the back street. The attendant stood shaking his head, surprised that Sowarth could even sit in the saddle as long as he had, let alone get the horse into a run. He went back inside

143

and put his shotgun against the door. He knew that before morning this fool would be back waking him up.

Five miles from town Jay Hurwood swung off the main trail and headed into slope timber. He soon found a cleared space between boulders and a thick dump of cottonwoods. Getting down, he worked the horse out of the shafts and then checked on Merle. She was fast asleep and didn't look like stir- ring for hours. Jay knew she had finished off the bottle of whiskey and only his touching her in the room had awakened her. But after the jogging in the rig, she would be out for as long as he wanted her to be. He pulled his saddle from the back of the rig and fixed it onto the horse. Then he swung up, checked Merle a second time and then let the horse pick its way back to the main trail.

Merle would sleep for hours, he was sure of that. But if she didn't, there was nowhere she could go, even if she knew where she was. There was food in back of the rig and a gun.

He got onto the trail again and headed back to Gabriel at a fast run, reaching the town no more than three hours after leaving it. He left the horse in a back street and made his way on foot to Doc Fogarty's cottage. He stayed in the darkness just off the porch until he was certain nobody had seen him, then he worked his way along the side of the house to the back. Getting to the back porch, he stopped and listened, but there was no sound but the wash of the wind against the vines on the porch. Gun in hand, Hurwood tried the back door. Locked. But soon he found an unlocked window. He eased the window up and climbed through, then he headed for the light showing in the passageway. Flattening himself against the wall, he peered into the room and saw where Lanny Sowarth had been sleeping only a few hours ago. The bed was empty.

Hurwood stood there, worry bringing deep ruts to his broad brow. He couldn't understand it. His check with Fogarty earlier in the afternoon had proved that Sowarth was in no condition to walk, let alone get out of bed and leave the cottage. Puzzled, Hurwood made his way through the house to Fogarty's room. But he found the room empty. Feeling panic beginning to take hold of him, Hurwood hurried to the front porch. He was in time to see Sheriff Plimpton and Doc Fogarty hurrying down the boardwalk towards the cottage. Drawing back inside, Hurwood cursed under his breath. Through some miracle Sowarth had got away from the place. Now the law was coming.

Hurwood hurried to the back of the house. He went across the yard and climbed the fence. He crouched then, his ears straining to pick up sound from the cottage. Shortly afterwards, Plimpton went into the house and after a few minutes came out.

On the porch Plimpton said, 'Well, you're right, Doc – he's gone. But I'm damned if I can believe he was capable of it.'

'He has hate in him,' was Fogarty's reply. Plimpton bade him goodnight and went back into the street. Jay Hurwood, sweating profusely now, walked to the back street and mounted his horse. He licked his dry lips and looked anxiously about him.

Where could Sowarth go?

He swung the horse about and rode down the back street. He had been seen leaving town, so what reason could he give for coming back? He decided no story he could make up would satisfy a worrier like Plimpton. He hit his horse into a run and sped from town. His intention was to wake Merle and get the rig going again. Then he'd put as many miles between himself and Lanny Sowarth as the night and the next day would permit. He'd change horses down near Temple Creek and press on for Montana. Up there in new country he'd soon get himself into a lucrative business.

146

*

Rod Plimpton thumped on Blake Durant's door until Durant opened up for him. By then both Hap Wheeler and Dave Crane had been wakened by the door pounding as were another four guests in the rooming house. Plimpton ignored all of them and said, 'Sowarth's skipped out on us.'

Blake looked curiously at Hap Wheeler and Crane who both frowned disbelievingly back at him.

Reading their doubts, Plimpton added, 'There ain't no mistake. I just searched Doc's place and checked on the stables. He got his horse, saddled up and rode out. Now what I want to know is where he went and why.'

Blake pulled his shirt about his shoulders, buttoned it up and tucked it in. Then he went inside and pulled on his gunbelt. Plimpton followed him into the room and after studying him heavily for a time, asked, 'So where the hell is he, Durant? What in blazes do you know about this anyway?'

'He's gone after Jay Hurwood,' Blake told him.

Plimpton gaped at him.

Blake eased the sheriff aside. 'If you want to know more, saddle up, Sheriff, and I'll meet you at the stables. I'll be ready to ride in five minutes.'

Plimpton looked from Durant to Wheeler and

then to Crane before going back into the doorway. 'What the hell's he after Hurwood for? And what the hell is Hurwood doing out there?'

'It's a long story and most of it doesn't fit, Sheriff,' Blake said impatiently. 'But when we find Hurwood and his woman, we'll probably find Lanny Sowarth.'

Crane asked, 'You want us to come along, Durant?'

Blake shook his head. 'No. The sheriff and I should be able to look after things. Get some rest.'

With that Blake went down the back steps, ignoring the faces peering at him from the doorways on the way. He went across the yard and strode into the livery stable horse yard, where Sundown immediately came running to him. Blake patted the horse and turned to find the attendant with a gun trained on him.

'Figured you was Sowarth come back, Durant. Hell, what's going on tonight, with everybody up and about and the law asking questions?'

Blake, not bothering to answer him, went inside and got his saddle. He had just saddled Sundown when Plimpton came riding into the yard. Blake swung up, turned Sundown away from the rail and kicked him into a run. Rod Plimpton let out a shout but Durant ignored him as he wheeled into the back street and then set the big black striding for the end of the town. Rod Plimpton followed as fast as his horse could go. Only when Durant slowed Sundown at the edge of town did Plimpton catch up with him.

Breathless, the lawman held his horse under a tight rein while Blake told him briefly what he thought had happened. Plimpton was astounded and could do no more than gape at him. Then Blake Durant was riding furiously through the night, heading along the trail towards Temple Creek, the trail the stable attendant had sworn was the one Lanny Sowarth had taken.

Lanny Sowarth was walking his horse, carefully nursing it and himself for what he considered was going to be a long ride. Wheeler had mentioned Hurwood driving a rig out of town, so he meant to travel in comfort. Lanny chuckled to himself. Comfort he'd get all right – six feet down.

The moonlight showed the trail ahead clearly and he picked the even sections where the horse's movement would not jolt him too much. Even so, his whole body ached and his head at times became furry and his sight blurred. But there was a force driving Lanny Sowarth on, and nothing would stop him until he found Hurwood and killed him.

Mile after mile he let the horse pick its way, and he was rounding a boulder – strewn slope when he heard movement to his right and then a woman called out, 'Jay, is that you? Jay?'

Lanny Sowarth pulled up his horse abruptly and saw her tall figure, with her skirt billowing out behind her, come running from the boulders. He drew his gun and trained it on her.

'Jay, where have you been? Why did you leave me here all alone? I woke up and was frightened out of my skin!'

Merle Butler came right up against the horse before she recognized Lanny Sowarth. Then she drew back, alarmed. Lanny came out of the saddle, knowing Jay Hurwood wasn't with her. Where was he?

He grasped her arm and pushed the gun against her temple. 'Ma'am, if you give me one spit of trouble I'll blow your pretty head off! You hear me?'

Merle was too terrified to answer, but she nodded and tried to break clear of him. But, despite his wounds, Lanny proved to be too strong for her. He let his horse go and pushed her in front of him. When they came to the clearing, he stood back and laughed.

'Seems the dude's run out on you, ma'am. What do you know about that now?'

'No,' Merle cried out adamantly. 'He wouldn't do that. I fell asleep. He probably decided to let me sleep.' Then she suddenly stiffened and backed away from him. 'He went back to town,' she said.

'Now why would he do that, little woman?' Lanny asked, the gun still trained on her.

'He . . . he wanted to kill you. He tried in town,' Merle exploded. Her only thought now was to save herself. Hurwood had left her out here at the mercy of trail scum like Sowarth, so she owed him nothing.

'Why would he want to kill me, ma'am?'

'Because . . . because he was frightened that you'd guessed he killed your brother. He came to town to arrange to sell his cattle and I told him about the attack you and your brother made on me in Sonora. I meant only to show him how dangerous it was to leave a woman alone and unprotected in these terrible frontier towns. He didn't say that he still had you both working for him, but when I saw you in town and recognized you, he tried to kill you. Then I made him leave town. I made him promise it was all over. Then just awhile back I woke up and heard you and thought . . . thought . . .'

Suddenly it was all too much for Merle Butler and she sank to the ground and sobbed into her hands. Lanny stood over her, watching her and saying nothing.

151

After a time, Merle composed herself and looked up fearfully, her face stained with tears. 'Don't hurt me. I never meant you any harm. It was Hurwood who killed your brother. And he meant to kill you this morning and again tonight when he went back to town.'

'He'll find me gone,' Lanny said tonelessly.

'Then he'll come back, Mr Sowarth – and he'll try to kill both of us. You have a horse. Let's harness it to the rig and keep going. His money is all here, under the seat. I saw him put it there back in town when he thought I wasn't watching. We can share it. It's a fortune.'

Lanny reached down and Merle looked fearfully up at him.

'No, don't touch me! I – I couldn't stand that.'

Lanny lashed out with his boot and sent her reeling onto her back. 'Couldn't stand my brother either, could you, woman?' he growled. 'Well, I ain't in no condition to take you, ma'am, not yet. But when I settle with Hurwood, I'm gonna lay up for some time and you're gonna nurse me back to health. Then by hell I'll have my fill of you. Now get up.'

Merle got slowly to her feet. She backed into the rig and Lanny Sowarth quickly tied her hands to the driving rail. Then he checked out the rig and was satisfied with its contents. Hurwood had stocked up for a trip through half the frontier. He settled down then, staring back over the trail he'd come.

He said, 'When did he leave, ma'am?'

'I don't know. I told you I was asleep.'

'Don't matter. I'll just rest up and wait for him. Soon as he comes, I'll kill him and then you and I will get to know each other a lot better. Now shut up and don't make one sound or you'll get the first bullet.'

Merle slumped against the side of the rig and began sobbing again. She had never felt more miserable. She hated Jay Hurwood now for being a fool as well as a murderer. But somehow there had to be a way out of this. She had Hurwood's money. All she had to do was get the better of this little cowhand. She stood there thinking deeply.

Jay Hurwood could hear them coming up the bench country. He couldn't tell how many there were, so he slid back into the timber on the slope and waited. Two horses finally appeared, caught clearly in the moonlight. Hurwood swore and sent his horse galloping again. He had to reach Merle and get going, not towards Temple Creek as he had planned, but back beyond Gabriel and south. There he could easily find a town to settle in. With Merle at his side, he would have the admiration of every-body. He'd have money to spend and plenty to make.

Hurwood had reached the bend in the trail where the boulders were clustered thickly. He was still well in front of the two riders. He swung off his horse, checked the trail thoroughly and then led the horse to the spot where he had left the rig. He saw Merle standing against it. She'd be as angry as all blue blazes, but he didn't mind that. In here, in cover, he'd be more than a match for anybody. And it could be that these two were just cowhands on the drift.

'Keep coming, Hurwood, you're just the little man I want to see.'

Jay Hurwood stopped dead in his tracks. He let go of his horse and stared into the darkness.

'Sowarth?' he asked tightly.

'You've got it dead right, Hurwood. Your little woman broke down and told me all about it. You killed Joe.'

'She's a damn liar! What the hell would I do that for?'

'Because she told you that Joe mauled her, which he did, but not the way she claimed. She looked for it, Hurwood, but that didn't matter a damn to you. You killed Joe and left me for Durant to finish. Only

Durant wasn't having any of me, was he, so you tried to gun me down in town.'

'No, Lanny. Let's talk it out and you'll see where you have it all wrong. Hell, if I'd wanted to kill you, I'd have had a dozen chances. Think of that.'

'I already thought of it, Hurwood, and I came up with the only answer – you left me for Durant, like I just said. Now come straight forward and keep them hands high. I'm gonna let this little woman see what kind of man she preferred to Joe and me.'

Hurwood shuffled forward slowly. Merle was astounded by the change in him. His whole body was trembling. He looked ready to faint.

Then Lanny Sowarth thumbed back the hammer of his gun and walked up to Hurwood. He put the gun muzzle against Hurwood's forehead and the cattle dealer let out a low groan. Lanny Sowarth pulled the trigger, the Colt kicked and Hurwood was thrown back. Merle screamed and struggled to free herself. The ropes cut into her skin but she didn't feel the pain.

Then Blake Durant and Rod Plimpton, hearing the shot, came charging into the clearing. Lanny Sowarth, about to release Merle from the ropes, swung around, his gun leveling. Plimpton was the first to come before him. In panic Lanny fired a shot. In the bad light, Rod Plimpton didn't know who was firing at him. And he didn't much care when the bullet burned past his face. He pumped three shots into Lanny Sowarth, the third hitting hit dead center in the forehead.

Sheriff Plimpton looked heavily at Durant from behind his desk. It was early morning and the bodies of Jay Hurwood and Lanny Sowarth had been brought back to town in the rig. Merle Butler had been taken to her room in the rooming house. Hap Wheeler and Dave Crane, hearing the commotion made getting the stunned Merle into her room, had gone with Plimpton and Blake Durant to the jailhouse. They stood against the wall now, listening as Durant told what had happened.

Crane said, 'Then Joe and Lanny started it all in Sonora.'

'Seems like,' Blake said.

'And you finished it in Gabriel,' Wheeler said.

Blake shook his head. 'No; the sheriff finished it. I had nothing against Lanny Sowarth.'

Blake Durant rose, tension still in him. The stupidity of needless death worried him. It happened so often out here on the frontier, where women were scarce and men wanted them badly. Joe Sowarth hadn't been able to control himself and Lanny Sowarth had died because of it.

'I'm turning in,' Durant said. 'I'll see you all later in the day.'

'I won't be down until after ten, that's for sure,' Plimpton said. And then, as Blake Durant walked to the doorway, he added, 'Durant, I reckon you pushed the issue all the way. You brought Hurwood into the open and you got Lanny Sowarth on the right track. When you saved his life in that laneway you opened the floodgates.'

Blake said nothing. He walked back to the rooming house with Hap and Crane and went to his room. Then, as he was closing the door, Merle Butler, who had been waiting in the darkness, slid against him and put her arms around his neck.

'Oh, Blake, I'm glad you came back,' she said. 'I just can't be alone tonight.'

Durant turned, releasing her grip on his neck. 'You can't stay here,' he said.

'But why, Blake? It was you who fixed everything up. I could never have stayed with Jay after what he did. And I was so terrified I was almost out of my mind until I saw you. I could have warned Sowarth but I didn't because I wanted you to come to me and save me. I think all along I had a premonition that you were the man for me. Jay was so jealous – and I gave him no cause to be.'

Blake opened the door as Merle clung to him.

157

'Blake, don't turn me out, please! I'll do anything you say.'

'For the moment go to bed,' Blake said. 'Maybe in the morning we'll talk about it. There's a lot to be cleared up.'

Merle licked her lips for several seconds, then nodded. 'In the morning then, Blake. We'll talk.'

Blake waited until her footsteps had faded down the passageway before he lit the lamp. Then he went to his bunk and rolled up his range pack. He checked out the room before leaving it and going into the yard where he had left Sundown.

As he saw it, Plimpton could tie up all the loose ends. Hap Wheeler and Dave Crane had each other and Wheeler wouldn't let Crane go off on his own. As for Merle Butler, there would be another man and another town and she had Hurwood's money to start with. If he went off with her, he knew he would eventually go bitter against the world. At any rate, his mind was still filled with the memory of another woman.

He swung up on Sundown and rode out of the yard. But as he crossed the laneway heading to the main street, he looked back on impulse. Hap Wheeler was leaning out of his window. Hap waved and Durant waved back. He liked Wheeler and Dave Crane. Perhaps someday they'd meet again.

But not in Gabriel. Gabriel had lost all interest for Blake Durant. There was just Sundown and another trail and time to forget his loss.

Turning into the main street, Blake rode past the jailhouse. Now another impulse forced him to look to the right. Rod Plimpton stood there, his gunbelt across his shoulder, his tin star gleaming in the moonlight.

Plimpton said, 'I hope you find whatever it is you're looking for, Durant. You asked me why I wore a badge. And there's your answer. I found mine.'

Blake gave him a nod and rode on. He went back over the same country he had travelled with Hurwood's herd. The country had dried out. He found the grave of the old woman and stood Sundown over it. He wondered what her life had been like and what had turned her head . . . how many people had loved her, how many had hated her? He looked skywards as drops of rain began to come down and then he rode off into the emptiness and the loneliness.